Dad, Tell Me a Story

How to Revive
the Tradition of Storytelling
with Your Children

John T. McCormick
with William & Connor McCormick

Dad, Tell Me a Story

How to Revive
the Tradition of Storytelling
with Your Children

Illustrated by
William, Connor, & John McCormick

Published by Nicasio Press
Freestone, California
www.NicasioPress.com

This book was typeset in Minion Pro
Book design by Constance King Design
Cover image and design by John T. McCormick © 2010

ISBN 978-0-9818636-3-4

In Memory of My Mother,

Virginia McCormick,

Who First Taught Me the Love of Storytelling

CONTENTS

◆

Cultural and Historical Stories

Growing Up Stories

ACKNOWLEDGEMENTS

I wish to thank my editors, Laura Duggan and Zu Vincent, for all their professional advice and support, and for teaching me so much about the art of writing and editing. I offer my additional thanks to Laura and Nicasio Press for assisting me with the publication and design of this book.

I also want to express my appreciation to my graphic designers, Patti Maurer and Connie King, for their expertise and artistry.

I especially wish to thank my beloved wife, Danna, not only for her assistance with the graphics and web marketing for this book, but for her loving support and patience during the five years it took me, together with our children, to write and illustrate the story behind our stories.

Finally, special thanks and love go to my children, William and Connor, for collaborating with me to write and illustrate this book. The stories in this book resulted from the creative interplay between my sons and me. I am very proud to be William and Connor's co-writer, co-illustrator, and best of all, their dad.

John T. McCormick
Washington, D.C.
September 2010

Introduction

LIKE MANY PARENTS, I enjoyed reading a bedtime story to my two sons each night after I tucked them in bed. When the story was over, we would turn out the lights, and I would lie next to them until they fell asleep. Sometimes we'd talk. Other times my sons would be so tired they were sound asleep before I could turn out the light.

Then one night after the lights were out, my oldest son, Will, who was about three years old at the time, asked for one more story. But this time, he asked me to tell him a "story with my mouth." That meant he wanted me to tell him one of my made-up stories, not someone else's story from a book. And so I did. I just made up a story about the first thing that came to mind. He loved it. So much so that he asked me the next night, "Dad, please tell me another story with your mouth."

Thus a storytelling tradition was born in our family. Will is twelve years old now, and his brother, Connor, is ten. Just about every night since that first night when Will asked me to tell him a story, I've made up an original story for my boys at bedtime. Of all the things I do for them, my storytelling is what they love the most. It has created a special bond between us, something that no one else does for them. They find that their day isn't complete without one of my stories.

Of course, not all the stories are literary prize winners. The first couple I tried were pretty awful. But my children didn't seem to care. What was important was that I had made up a special story just for them, one that no one else in the world had ever been told!

After a while, I became a lot better at making up stories. I came up with a formula, and even a few tricks to use whenever I got storyteller's block. It even got fairly easy. When my friends marveled at how I could make up a new story every night, night after night, I told them that it wasn't that difficult. They could do it too.

And so can you. That's the idea for this book. It contains a selection of some of the stories I made up for my children, or perhaps it is more correct to say, that we made up together. For you see, that is the secret of storytelling with your children. Get them involved. A story means so much more to them when they can contribute to it, and be a part of it. Besides, on nights when you can't think of an idea for a story, you'll need their help to come up with a new one.

When I see how important our storytelling is in my sons' lives, I scratch my head to think how much our television and video-oriented society has lost in terms of the personal connections storytelling brings. Before the invention of such technological marvels as television, DVDs, computer games, MP3s, and now "I-everythings," a family's evening was built around storytelling (along with letter writing, playing music or games, and reading aloud from books and poetry—other lost traditions). This oral tradition was passed down from generation to generation, and many of the epic stories we have today originated from this tradition until someone finally wrote them down.

The secret to good storytelling is just that—telling a good story. All you need is an eager audience (that's the easy part), and a good idea for a story (that can sometimes be a little harder). Your children will be your audience; they're *always* ready to be entertained. As for ideas, each chapter and many of the stories in this book begin with notes offering suggestions and examples for plots, themes, beginnings, endings, morals, and storytelling games, along with some parenting insights.

Instead of offering storytelling how-to's to either parents or children, these notes focus on the interactive process of storytelling between parent and child. Parents are encouraged to make up stories with, rather than just for, their children. The results are often unpredictable, but always entertaining.

If you're not yet ready to start telling your own stories, you can always warm up by reading to your children some of the stories in this book. The book contains twenty-five of the actual stories that my sons and I created together. As you gain confidence, try making up stories with your children using some of the storytelling ideas and techniques that my own children and I developed. Before long, you and your kids will have your own family tradition of made-up, just for fun, oral storytelling.

How to Get Started

WHEN IT COMES TO STORYTELLING, there should be no hard and fast rules. So I'm not going to give you any. At least I'm not going to call them rules; just helpful hints or suggestions which you'll find here and throughout the book. And the number one suggestion I have for telling a good, original story is to be spontaneous. That might sound a little cliché, but it's true. Spontaneity is the key to a good story. It's not always easy to be spontaneous when you're tired, sick, or a little cranky. So how do you invoke spontaneity? With a couple of simple tricks.

Start the story with the very *first* idea that comes into your mind. Don't put off starting your story while you wait for a better idea to come along. And certainly don't play it safe by trying to think through your story from beginning to end before you even start. If you do that, you'll try to make the story perfect and it will never get off the ground. (Either that, or your child will fall asleep before you even get going.) In fact, the best stories result when you begin a story without a clue as to how it will end.

An even better way to start your story is to *ask your child* what he or she wants the story to be about. This gets your child involved in the story right from the beginning, which will help keep your child's interest piqued. It's also better to have your child come up with the subject because it forces you out of your comfort zone. If you pick the subject, you may be tempted to tell a story similar to one you've already heard. That's okay, but telling a story on a new topic will squeeze out all your creative juices. The very best stories are new and unexpected. And dare I say again, spontaneous.

And when I say the very first idea that comes up, I mean just that. Your child may say, "I want a story about aardvarks." Then tell a story about aardvarks, even if you have no idea what an aardvark is. Invent a story about a baby aardvark separated from her parents who has to figure out what she is and how to survive on her own.

The idea can be very serious or very silly. It doesn't matter. If it doesn't match your mood at the time, all the better. By prompting you to tell a serious story when you're happy, or a silly story when you're down, going with the first idea that comes to mind will draw out more of your creativity and imagination. (And if you're feeling sad, a funny story might cheer you up!) One Friday night, after my family and I had a very festive evening at a neighborhood restaurant, I asked my son what he wanted his bedtime story to be about.

I thought he would ask me for a funny story about Simi. Simi was the fictional lizard we created together from a little stuffed yellow lizard in a McDonald's Happy Meal for Kids. I use this over-the-top silly voice when speaking for Simi in my stories, and it never fails to put my son into side-splitting hysterics.

Instead, much to my surprise, my son asked me why people have wars. Whoa! Where did that come from? What a downer idea for a story, I thought at the time. But it forced me to come up with a way to answer his question with a thoughtful and imaginative story, while at the same time not overloading him with anxiety or sadness about so serious a subject. Sometimes, in discussing serious subjects with your children, it's better to answer their questions with a parable or a story, rather than an explanation.

What to do if you get stuck

If you and your child are still stumped for a good story idea, you can always try a tried and true formula. There's nothing original about this formula. Writers have been following it since time began because it comes naturally to storytellers. It's so natural and straightforward that I discovered I was using this formula when making up my own stories without even knowing that I was actually doing so. Here's how it goes.

Step One: Have your child pick a person, animal, object, place, or idea as the lead subject for your story. (Remember, tell your child to pick the very first thing that pops into her head.)

Step Two: Describe the main character in more detail, perhaps by telling what makes him so special. In other words, set the scene.

Step Three: Create tension in your story. Describe some challenge or problem for your main character.

Step Four: Resolve the challenge or problem in a way that is humorous, enlightening, or teaches a lesson. Be sure to ask your child what the main character should do to resolve this problem or challenge.

Here's an example of a story I made up quickly with one of my sons as I was typing.

The Dog and the Three Country Cats

Step One: *There once was a dog who loved to chase cats. All the cats called him Ambush, because he loved to sneak up on an unsuspecting cat, and without warning, scare her with a series of high-pitched barks. "Ruff, ruff, ruff, ruff!" barked Ambush. "Screech!" shrieked the cat, as she jumped straight up into the air. "Ha! Ha! Ha!" laughed Ambush at the poor cat's expense.*

Step Two: *Then, one day, a new family moved into the neighborhood with three cats named Powder-puff, Snowflake, and Cuddles. "They must be real scaredy cats with wimpy names like those," said Ambush with glee. "I'm gonna have lots of fun bossing these new kitties around."*

Step Three: *But there was one thing Ambush didn't know. These new cats weren't ordinary cats. They were country cats. Country cats are a lot tougher than city cats. They're used to dealing will all sorts of ornery varmints—snakes, foxes, and sometimes, coyotes. Powderpuff, Snowflake, and Cuddles, despite their softy names, knew how to take care of themselves.*

Step Four: *One day, Ambush decided to play his usual trick on the cats, who were sunning themselves in their front yard. Ambush crept forward on his belly. Closer and closer until, "Ruff! Ruff! RUFF!"*

Ambush stood there with his tail wagging and a grin on his face, waiting to see what always happened next—cats screeching in terror as they jumped straight into the air. He especially loved to see their fur shoot out in all directions, as if the cats had gotten their tails stuck in an electric socket.

Instead, Powderpuff, Snowflake, and Cuddles calmly rose to their feet and walked over to Ambush. They unsheathed their claws as if they were switchblade knives. "Pfft, pfft, pfft!" went the sound of their whirling claws as they carved up Ambush's nose. After they were done, Ambush's nose looked like a pin cushion. Ambush whimpered and moaned, and ran away as fast as he could with his tail tucked between his legs.

Ambush got a new nickname after that day. Mouse. Mouse, because from then on, he was as quiet as one. Never again did he ambush or scare a cat. Mouse had learned his lesson. Although they may look alike, not all cats are the same. And Mouse wasn't going to take any more chances by picking a fight with one of those country cats!

(The End)

Even when you come up with a good idea for a story, you're probably going to get stuck part way through. Many times I've gotten to the halfway point with no idea how to finish on a high note or with a flourish. What do you do? Here are a couple of suggestions.

If you get stuck part way through the story, stall for time by asking your child, "Guess what happened next?" Can you predict what your child will say? I can, because kids *always* say the same thing at first: "I don't know." But don't let your child off the hook. Ask them to guess. Ask them for the first idea that pops into their mind.

If your child gives you a good idea for a direction to take your story, use it. She'll be very excited to hear that you liked her idea and that she's contributed to the story. Even if your child's idea doesn't work, the pause will give you time to think of a new direction for your story. Or perhaps your child's idea isn't on the mark, but close. You can say, "That's a good way to end the story, but here's a similar idea I came up with. Let me know what you think."

Storytelling games

As you gain confidence coming up with story ideas, try playing storytelling games with your kids. For example, have each of your children pick one object, person, or animal to be included in the story, until four story characters are chosen. (And if you have an only child, you can take turns with her picking the characters.) The four characters don't have to have anything in common. In fact, it makes for a better story (and more of a challenge) if they don't. Then combine the different characters into one story. You have to be on your toes to pull this off, because, knowing kids, they'll probably come up with story characters that couldn't be more dissimilar if they tried.

In our family, we have a shorthand name for this type of storytelling—combination stories. All I have to do is shout "combination story!" and my sons Will and Connor start yelling out characters. For example, one time they came up with such unlikely subjects as (1) a phoenix, (2) a tooth, (3) a treasure of gold, and (4) a mountain. The story that resulted, "The Phoenix and the Volcano of Gold," is included in this book. Judge for yourself how well we did in making up a story on the fly using subjects that initially appeared to have nothing in common.

After you've become a little more practiced in telling combination stories, you and your children can have a friendly game of speed storytelling. Everyone takes a turn at making up a story involving the four characters (kids always have Mom or Dad go first), but each must tell the story as quickly as possible. That way, there's no time for storyteller's block. The need to tell the story quickly (remember, as fast as you can) often breaks up any inhibitions or creative logjams in the brain. One of my speed stories, "I Want My Magic TV," is also included in the book.

One little warning; (but don't worry)

Don't expect all your stories to be met with applause, or even the satisfied sigh of a child as she rolls over and falls sleep after you solemnly pronounce, "The End." Many of my friends marvel that I've been telling my children original stories every night for several years. "Making up a story is the easy part," I say. "The hard part is making it a *good* story."

That's right; be forewarned. Not only will your kids eventually want an original story every night, they may also expect it to be a very good story as well. After some of my more mediocre efforts, I've heard complaints such as, "Dad, that was lame." Or, "Dad, that was too short." I sometimes tell my friends that I'm not so much grooming my children to be future writers or storytellers, but critics!

But don't despair. Accept with grace that you're not going to come up with a prize-winning story every night. At the same time, take heart in the fact that an original story you've made up just for your children—no matter its literary quality—is often more special to them than a professionally written story they might read. You'll be surprised how, even after several years have gone by, your child will still remember most of the stories, good or bad, that you've told them.

The difference between reading stories from a book and inventing your own is similar to that between stand-up comedy and improv. The comedian prepares his material before a performance, then stands up and delivers his routine to an audience. Even if the comedian's delivery is good and his material funny, the routine is still rehearsed.

Not so with improvisation. An improviser makes up his material on the spot, feeding off of others, picking up ideas for comedy bits from his real-time interaction with other performers and the audience. The result can be spell-binding, since it is based on creativity in the moment. If the improviser is funny, the audience appreciates the performance all the more because of its spontaneity. And if the improviser bombs, even better. With improv, the attempt is often funnier than the pre-packaged delivery of the stand-up comedian.

Some final advice

I have one last suggestion that goes hand-in-hand with being spontaneous. The more fantastical you can be, the more creative your story is, the more your child will love it. You can never overdo a story with your kids. Think soap opera plot lines (without the racy parts), or even better, high opera. In the movie *Amadeus,* there's a scene in which Mozart's friend, a wandering musician, theater manager, and schemer named Emanuel Schikaneder, tries to convince Mozart to write an opera for him and his company. Schikaneder tells Mozart not to write another court opera that Vienna's snobby elite will ignore, but one for the common people. Says Schikaneder, "The more fantastic, the better. That's what people want. Fantasy." Mozart is persuaded, and goes on to write one of the most fantastical, imaginative operas in the history of music, *The Magic Flute.* It's filled with dragons, witches, and all sorts of colorful characters. Schikaneder was right. The common people of Vienna loved the opera when it premiered, as do people today—especially children—because it's so over the top.

To sum up, no pre-planned stories. Be spontaneous. Tell a story about the very first thing that comes into your head. If you get stuck, ask your child for help. "Can you guess what happened next?" He'll give you a good idea, or at the very least, it will allow you to stall for time until you can think of a new direction or ending. And of course, be as creative as you can. In the fictionalized words of Mozart's friend, "The more fantastic, the better."

Author's Note

The bedtime stories I've collected for this book fall into four categories: Animal Stories, Adventures and Folk Tales, Cultural and Historical Stories, and finally, Growing Up Stories. The stories mirror the growth and development of children, progressing in order from those that especially delight younger children to those that reflect maturing children's concerns and questions about the world around them. Young children cherish tales about animals and nature, while their slightly older siblings and friends love stories about fantasy, adventure, and faraway cultures and places. More mature children love fantasy and adventure stories too, but also identify with stories about growing up.

Parents are encouraged to read these stories with their children to answer questions or explain new words or concepts. Teaching is, after all, a very important part of storytelling. Most of the stories in this book suggest a moral or lesson learned. Ask your own children what they would've done in the main character's place. Feel free to suggest other ways the main character might deal with a problem or challenge. Don't worry if your endings are corny or a little obvious. Remember, no story is corny to a young child listening to it for the first time.

ANIMAL STORIES

CM
WM
Jm
2010

The Little Green Beetle

Author's Note: Most children's first stories are about animals. Animals and nature hold a special place in children's imagination and affections, and often continue to do so long after they've grown up. Animals amaze, comfort, delight, inspire, amuse, and best of all, offer countless ideas for stories.

In case you are wondering, here is one of the very first animal stories that I made up for my own sons when they were very young.

ONCE THERE WAS a little beetle walking through a field. There were two things about this beetle that made him quite extraordinary. First, he was one determined, tough little beetle. One could easily see this by the way he walked confidently across the field. Chest out, one leg after the other, afraid of no creature or thing. He looked more like a tough old bulldog than some puny insect.

The second extraordinary thing about this beetle was his color. He was lime green, covered in orange spots. Not just any green, but *neon* lime green. The kind of green that glows in the dark. In fact, even though this beetle was very tiny and was walking in a large field, another animal could easily spot him a mile away. Especially a predator. A predator is an animal that eats other animals for food.

As the beetle was marching along, a very hungry crow dropped from the sky and landed next to him.

Crow said, "And what do we have here?"

The beetle said nothing. He didn't even look at the crow, but stared intently ahead in the direction he was going.

"Too scared to speak, huh?" said Crow.

No reply from the beetle.

The crow began to walk alongside the beetle, who was still trudging ahead. "That's some green jacket you're sporting! I spotted you miles away. If I were you, I might want to wear something a little less noticeable."

"Really?" said Beetle, speaking up for the first time.

"Really," Crow said. "Just seeing that juicy green color made my mouth water. In fact, I dropped down to see if you tasted as good as you look."

"I wouldn't eat me if I were you," Beetle said.

"Why not?" asked Crow.

"Well," said Beetle, "have you ever seen a beetle with such a bright green shell before?"

"No."

"And have you ever seen a beetle with such bright orange spots before?"

"No."

"That's because I'm poisonous," said Beetle.

"What?" Crow looked confused.

"There is poison in my body and shell," explained Beetle. "The poison gives me bright colors and unusual markings to warn predators to stay away."

"Wait a second," said Crow. "You're bluffing so I won't eat you."

"If you're so sure," said Beetle, "then go ahead and eat me."

Crow hesitated. He muttered to himself. "I know this little beetle is bluffing, and he looks mighty tasty. But if I'm wrong and I eat this little bug, I could be one dead bird."

At last, Crow sighed. "You're too puny a snack to risk getting poisoned," he said. "Especially when there are so many bigger, more delicious, and less mouthy bugs in the woods. So long, little beetle," called Crow, as he lifted his wings and took off toward the surrounding forest.

The little green beetle said not a word in reply, but kept on walking. After a few moments, he paused and laughed aloud. "They fall for that one every time!"

Dude, the Homeless Hermit Crab

Author's Note: The best way to quiet rowdy kids at bedtime is to tell a story with a catchy opening. Just as a fisherman sets the hook to catch a fish, a storyteller can use a clever opening line or paragraph to grab a child's attention and hold it for the duration of the story. Several stories in this book, "A Pirate Never Forgets," "The City of Frozen Canals," "The Lost Guitar," and "Dude, the Homeless Hermit Crab" below, provide examples of good beginnings. They draw the listener in by painting a vibrant story scene, describing a magnetic main character, or introducing a seemingly insolvable problem or puzzle.

ONCE UPON A TIME, THERE WAS A LITTLE HERMIT CRAB named Dude. Dude wasn't just little. He was the smallest hermit crab on the beach. Sometimes the bigger crabs picked on him, but that didn't bother Dude. He laughed off the bullying, and made a joke about how small he was. Dude had a great outlook on life. Nothing ever bothered him.

Except for one thing. He was so small he was always the last crab to find a new home for the next growing season. Hermit crabs don't make their own shells. They have to borrow the discarded shells of other sea creatures.

One hot morning, as Dude was searching for a new shell, he saw something that made him think his luck had finally changed. There, nestled in a sand dune ahead, sparkled a beautiful conch shell. A palatial home if Dude ever saw one. Dude walked sideways up to the shell, and lifted one edge so he could slip inside. But his elation soon turned to disappointment. Another crab had gotten there first and was safely holed up inside.

"Hey, buddy," growled the intruder, "go get your own shell."

Dude turned away in disappointment. He crawled about on the beach for several more hours, until he spied a small welk shell lying abandoned on the beach. Not as big as the shell he'd seen before, but just as beautiful. Best of all, it didn't have an owner.

14

"Don't get your hopes up yet," said a cautious Dude. He inched up to the shell, and gave it a poke with his claw. Nothing happened. Another claw poke. Then a sniff. No crab inside this shell. Did he dare? He picked up the shell and crawled inside. It fit! Comfy, yet plenty of room. The perfect home.

Or so he thought. A larger crab sidled up to Dude. "What are you doing in my shell?" said the bully.

"Your shell?" said Dude. "It was mine first."

"Well, it's mine last," said the bully. He yanked the shell away from Dude and slung it onto his own back. "A little snug," the bully said. "But it will have to do. Don't want to be caught out in this hot sun without a shell."

As the bully slinked away, Dude squinted into the blazing sun. It sure was hot. "The bully's right," said Dude. "If I don't find a shell soon, the sun is going to broil me alive."

Dude became worried. He searched frantically for a shell. Just when he thought things couldn't get worse, they did. Dude heard above him a series of high-pitched calls and yelps. He looked up into the sky. Seagulls! "They'll make a quick meal of me if I don't find a home soon."

Dude had to improvise. He found an object on the beach that just might work. He crawled inside and *ahhhh!* Very cushy and well-lit. His new home was made of soft brown paper, with someone's half-eaten lunch inside. Sure, it wasn't exactly a shell, but it would protect him from the sun and hungry birds.

Just as Dude was getting comfortable—yikes! His new home was lifted into the air and crumpled around him. The very next moment he was spinning claws over tail through the air. He landed with a *plunk* on hard metal. Dude crawled out of his crumpled home to find . . . "Oh no!" He was in a big steel cage, like a common criminal thrown in jail.

Dude tried to climb out. He slid back down to the bottom of the cage. The sides were so steep and tall. "What am I going to do?" said Dude. "I can't crawl through the holes in the sides of this cage. They're too small. And I can't dig my way down, the bottom is metal. If don't find a way out soon, I'll starve."

Overhead, Dude heard again the calls of the seagulls. Soon one of those gulls would see him and make him his next meal.

What could Dude do? Just then an empty soda bottle sailed through the air and hit Dude on the head. "Eureka!" he cried. He now knew exactly what he must do in order to escape his prison.

Nothing.

That's right, nothing. Dude looked through his prison bars. He saw lots of people playing on the beach and swimming in the ocean. He would simply wait until the people threw enough garbage into his cage so he could climb up the trash pile and escape. Ingenious!

Dude was lucky, because it was a crowded beach day. The more people there are, the more trash they throw away. "People sure are messy," he thought. They threw all sorts of stinky, messy trash into his cage. Newspapers, magazines, empty bottles, yucky diapers. The kids were the worst, because they tossed their half-eaten food into the cage. "How do they eat this stuff?" said Dude. In no time, Dude's cage was filled to the brim with trash.

Dude climbed up the litter pile until he was at the top. "Wow, that's a long way down," he said as he peered over the cage rim. He was about to jump off the top and onto the sand below, and freedom, when he had a nagging thought. "I still don't have a new home for this season. What am I going to do now?"

At that moment, another piece of trash came spinning threw the air, hitting Dude again on the head. But this wasn't just another piece of trash. It was a special piece of trash. The most beautiful piece of trash Dude had ever seen. A shiny metal can! It was a small can, which would make a perfect home for Dude. Dude grabbed it in his big pincher, jumped off the trashcan, and parachuted onto the sand with the can in tow. He crawled inside. It covered him perfectly and kept him safe from hungry birds. And when a big storm came up, Dude could always turn it over, jump inside, and use it as a lifeboat in case the beach flooded.

It also attracted lots of attention. Not from the big male hermit crabs, the can was too small for them to make a home. It caught the eye of a female crab named Daisy. When Dude saw Daisy, his eyes stood straight up on their stalks. Daisy was the most beautiful hermit crab in the world.

Daisy was also very impressed with Dude. Never before had she seen a hermit crab with a home so shiny and silvery. This was the most attention Dude had ever received from a female crab. And all because, instead of seeing trash in other peoples' throw-aways, Dude saw a home.

The Plant Eaters Fight Back!

Author's Note: Start a story with your child about a subject they've recently discussed in school or seen on television or at the movies. My children are always fascinated by trips to the zoo, or by TV shows about Africa's jungles and plains. Begin with a dialogue that sets the scene of the story for them. For example:

Africa. Vast grasslands filled with herds of just about every type of animal imaginable. Reptiles, birds, insects, and of course, mammals.

There are two kinds of mammals: meat eaters and plant eaters. Another word for meat eaters is carnivores. And plant eaters? They're herbivores.

What are some meat eaters? Lions, cheetahs, leopards, and crocodiles. They are some of Africa's most famous carnivores.

What about plant eaters? There are lots of them. Giraffes, zebras, gazelles, hippos, rhinos, and monkeys. Although some types of monkeys have been known to eat meat, they're included with the herbivores in this story, which is about a bunch of plant eaters in East Africa who had a big problem.

ON THE SERENGETI PLAINS OF EAST AFRICA, there was a herd of plant eaters living peacefully together. This herd included giraffes, cape buffalos, zebras, rhinos, peacocks, hippopotamuses, all sorts of gazelles, and even a few monkeys. While they had enough food to eat and water to drink most of the year, they still lived a pretty rough life. Because of the predators. Meat eaters—like cheetahs, leopards, crocodiles, hyenas, and especially the lions—were constantly hunting the plant eaters.

When the meat eaters were hungry, they stalked the plant eaters, circling them to pick off the weakest animals. They went especially for the old, the young, and the sick. The parents among the plant eaters worried about their babies, and the babies worried about their parents. The plant eaters had no rest.

One day, the plant eaters decided they'd had enough. They met under a big acacia tree to talk about what to do. The giraffe led the meeting because she was the tallest and could talk over everyone else. "Does anyone have any ideas?" asked the giraffe in a commanding voice. No one answered. The giraffe grew frustrated. "Doesn't someone have a plan for protecting us from the meat eaters?"

Still, no one answered. The plant eaters just looked at one another. Then, they began arguing among themselves over how to fight the meat eaters.

"Pipe down," shouted the giraffe. "It does no good arguing among ourselves." This did little to quiet the plant eaters. Finally, the giraffe let out a piercing whistle. That got everyone's attention. The animals grew quiet.

"That's better," said the giraffe. "Why don't we do this? Why don't we go around the circle and each of us will say what we do to protect ourselves from predator attacks? Who will start?"

"I will," said the monkey. The monkey was always a jabberer. "One of us sits in a tree as a lookout. Whenever the lookout sees a predator, he shouts out a warning to everyone else. All the other monkeys then hightail it to safety in a nearby tree."

"That's great," said the giraffe, her ears twitching in excitement. "Who's next?"

No one volunteered. "How about you, Gazelle?" asked the giraffe.

The gazelle was very shy. In a soft voice he said, "We gazelles really don't do anything special. As soon as we smell or hear or see a lion, we just run as fast as we can."

The giraffe said, "That is very special. Gazelles are some of the fastest animals on the Serengeti. Running is a very good defense against predator attack."

"How about you, Zebra," asked the giraffe. "What do you do?"

"I run too," said the zebra. "But I also use my stripes as camouflage. I run very close to the other zebras in my herd. The sight of all our stripes swirling together makes it hard for lions to single out one of us for attack. The lions sometimes get confused. All those stripes moving in and out of focus makes them dizzy. It's pretty funny to watch a dizzy lion stumbling back and forth after he has tried to catch one of us!" Everyone laughed.

The giraffe said, "I run, too. But if I get the chance, I give the predators a kick in the chops with one of my hooves." The other animals cheered. "So do we," said the zebras, kicking their back legs high to show the others.

The giraffe asked the rhino, "Do you ever run from predators?"

The rhino's lip curled in a snarl. "Never. If one of those lions tries to bother me, I charge. The sight of my big horn makes them run away pretty fast."

"We have powerful horns too," said the cape buffalo. "But our best defense is to gather our calves in a group. Then the adults circle them for protection. We create a fortress around them, all bristling with horns and bad tempers. That scares off the predators!"

Giraffe asked, "Hippo, what do you do about lions?"

The hippo, who was always rather grumpy, yawned, "Nothing."

"What do you mean, 'nothing'?" asked the giraffe.

"The lions never bother us," said the hippo. "We could care less."

"Well, don't the predators ever try to harm your babies?" pressed the giraffe.

The hippo thought for a moment. "Sometimes the crocs try to grab one of the young hippos when the adults aren't paying attention."

"So what do you do then?"

"I charge the crocs," snorted the hippo, "that's what I do. If I catch one, I bite and stomp him. And that's the end of that croc."

"Wait a second," interrupted the peacock in a shrill voice. "Not all of us have horns to charge a lion, or teeth to bite a crocodile. Each of us here is very different. I don't see any way for us to come up with a plan where we can all be safe."

"Oh yes, there is," said the giraffe. "Listening to you has given me a great idea. Here is what we do . . . ." She bent down to whisper her plan to them. The other plant eaters gathered close to hear what the giraffe had to say. Once she had finished, they talked together in hushed, excited voices.

The gruff hippo said, "You call that a plan?"

"You got a better one?" said the wildebeest.

The ostrich was cautious. "Can we really do all that?"

"Why not," said the warthog. "What do we have to lose?"

"This won't scare Brutus," said the antelope.

"Who's Brutus?" asked the monkey.

"He's the top lion," replied the gazelle. "And the meanest, scariest predator of all."

The giraffe calmed everyone. "I've got just the answer for Brutus. Listen up."

The group talked some more. Finally, they agreed to the plan. The only question was, would it work?

The plant eaters didn't have to wait long to find out. The very next day, they got their chance.

Late in the afternoon, a pride of lions approached and started stalking the plant eaters. The lionesses led the way, followed by Brutus, the leader of the pride. Brutus sported a great blond mane and was the biggest lion on the Serengeti. The lionesses crouched with their bellies near the ground, careful to stay downwind so the plant eaters couldn't pick up their scent.

In fact, the plant eaters wouldn't even have known the lions were approaching had it not been for several of the monkeys acting as lookouts in a nearby tree. When the monkeys spotted the lions creeping in the tall grass, they called out a warning to all the plant eaters. "EEEeeeeEEEEEEeeeeEEEE!" they shouted, and pointed in the direction of the lions.

"Quick," shouted the giraffe, "circle around me just the way we planned!"

The cape buffalo gathered the most vulnerable members of the herd—the young, the old, and the sick—into a tight circle. Those animals with horns, teeth, and tusks, such as the buffaloes, rhinos, and the hippo, formed a wall around them for protection.

Then, the giraffe gave a command to the zebras, gazelles, antelopes, and ostriches. "Fast runners, you know what to do!"

The fast runners ran around and around the rest of the herd. The dust they kicked up drifted into the lions' faces. It irritated their eyes. It made them cough and sneeze. Worse for the lions, the sight of all the plant eaters' different spots and stripes swirling in and out of the dust cloud made them dizzy.

Just when the lions were losing confidence, Brutus charged forward. "Everyone, listen to me," he growled. "The plant eaters are making fun of us. They hope to confuse and trick us. But the trick will be on them. They're no match for our combined strength, teeth, and claws. Let's attack!" The other lions picked up the roar. Together they charged toward the heart of the plant eaters' herd.

But the plant eaters didn't move. The giraffe watched the lions charge. She waited. And waited. At last, the giraffe gave the order, "Horned animals . . . CHARGE!"

The buffaloes, rhinos, and the hippo walked at first. Then they trotted. When the giraffe shouted a second command, "Horns down," they broke into an all-out charge.

The buffaloes lowered their heads and shook their giant horns from side to side. The rhinos bucked their horns up and down in a stabbing motion. The hippo opened his mouth wide, exposing nasty looking tusks.

What a collision it was! When the rhinos and buffaloes hit the lions with their horns, the lions went flying. Even the hippo, who, to tell the truth, had a little trouble keeping up, managed to bite Brutus on the behind. Brutus and the other lions wasted no time getting out of there. No meal was worth the kicking, biting, goring, dizziness, and confusion they had to endure to get it.

The plant eaters couldn't believe their eyes. They—humble plant eaters—had chased away some of the biggest, baddest predators in all of Africa. Even Brutus proved no match for them. All at once, they broke into cheers. The monkeys cackled. The rhinos snorted. The gazelles and antelopes kicked their heels. The peacocks spread their plumage. Even the hippo cracked a toothy smile.

That night, they threw a big party for themselves. They enjoyed all their favorite foods and drink, and danced the night away underneath the starry skies. But even while they partied, they still had the monkeys keep a lookout in the trees . . . just in case.

The Raven Who Talked Too Much

Author's Note: Take an old favorite and give it a new twist.

You've probably heard Aesop's fable about the crow and the fox. In that story, a crow was sitting in a tree, eating a piece of meat. Along came a fox, who wanted the piece of meat for himself. So he praised the crow, telling the crow how beautiful and regal he was. And then the fox laid the trap.

"You could be the king of birds, if only you could sing." The crow fidgeted on the branch. Down below, the fox sighed and looked up at the crow in expectation. When the crow could stand it no longer, he opened his beak and screeched, "Caw! Caw! Caw! Who says I can't sing?" The piece of meat, of course, fell out of the crow's beak. The fox gobbled it up and ran away screaming, "You may have a voice, my dear crow. But you need something else to become king . . . a brain!"

On those occasions when you get stuck for an idea, pick a well-known story or fable, and add a few twists to it. Here's one about a raven, who like Aesop's crow, was a little too sure of himself.

ON A BEAUTIFUL SUMMER'S DAY, a group of people gathered for a picnic. They spread out their tablecloth on the cool green grass and opened up their picnic basket full of delicious food. They were all very hungry and couldn't wait to eat.

But the picnickers weren't the only ones in the neighborhood who were hungry.

On the branch of a nearby tree sat a bothersome raven. "Caw! Caw! Caw!" called the raven. The raven hoped that his noisemaking would make the humans go away, leaving him alone to enjoy the picnic food. But those pesky humans wouldn't be shooed away.

Then the raven had an idea. A black snake was sunning himself on a nearby rock. The raven knew that most humans are afraid of snakes. The raven flew over to the rock. Before the snake knew what happened, the raven picked it up in his claws, flew back over to the

24

picnickers, and dropped the snake right in the middle of their picnic blanket.

The next sound the raven heard was screaming. The picnickers rushed back to their car, jumped in, and drove away. They were so scared that they left their entire picnic lunch behind.

The raven couldn't believe his good fortune. He had come up with the idea to scare the people away with the snake, but even he was surprised it had worked so well. The raven was very proud of himself. "I'm so smart," he kept telling himself. After a while, he decided to tell all the animals in the forest how smart he had been.

"Caw! Everyone. Caw!" shouted the raven. "Come here. I have an important announcement to make." All the animals, insects, and birds in the neighborhood gathered around the picnic blanket to listen to the raven. The raven told everyone exactly what had happened. He was very sure to remind them how smart he was.

Meanwhile, all the forest creatures started eyeing the delicious food. One by one, each animal ate a small morsel of food while the raven was speaking. When the raven took a breath, a squirrel said, "Oh, yes, raven. What a smart bird you are." A frog chimed in. "Yes, indeed, you are the smartest animal in the land. Would you please tell us the story again?"

The forest creatures got the raven to repeat his story five times. By then, they had eaten the entire picnic, right under the nose—or shall we say the beak—of the raven. The rabbits stripped the celery of their leaves. The turtles gobbled up the hard boiled eggs. The ants carried off all the grapes. The raven was so enthralled with his story, he didn't even notice. Even the snake got to eat a big link of salami. At last the raven stopped talking and looked around. Everyone and everything was gone, including the picnic.

Flapjack the Beaver

Author's Note: Every parent has, at times, resorted to reverse psychology. The following story illustrates that kids will do their chores once you convince them that work can sometimes be as fun as play.

THERE WAS A HAPPY LITTLE BEAVER named Flapjack. He was called Flapjack because he liked to flatten mud balls into pancakes with his tail. Flapjack then tossed them into the air like a short order cook flipping pancakes.

The only problem with Flapjack was that he liked to play more than he liked to work. That's not a good way for a beaver to be. Beavers are some of the hardest working animals around. While the other beavers were cutting trees, stacking logs, and scooping up mud to fill in the spaces between the logs in their dam, Flapjack was happily juggling his mud pancakes all by himself on the riverbank.

"Hey, Flapjack, get over here and help," cried Waddles, one of the other beavers. Although Waddles got his nickname because he ate too many fish during breaks, he was the hardest worker of the group. Flapjack replied with a bored look on his face, "Maybe tomorrow." Flapjack wasn't being mean. He just had more fun playing in the bright sunshine than working on the dam.

One day, Waddles and a few of the other beavers grew so frustrated with Flapjack that they went to see Flapjack's mom, a grey-haired beaver named Mattie. Waddles told Mattie about the problems they were having with Flapjack, and how they were doing all the work while he played. "It's just not fair," said Waddles.

Mattie sighed. She knew they had to find a way to get Flapjack to help with the work. It really wasn't fair to the other beavers. However, she also knew her son. Flapjack didn't respond well when he was told what to do. Mattie had to find a way to make Flapjack want to help with the dam building.

Mattie said to the other beavers, "You're absolutely right. We do need to find a way to get Flapjack to pitch in. But we need to change Flapjack without him knowing what we're up to. I'll come to the riverbank tomorrow morning and see if I can help. Okay?"

"Okay," said Waddles and the other beavers. They trudged home to get a good night's rest for tomorrow's workday.

The next morning, Mattie strolled down to the riverbank. While Waddles and the other beavers were building a dam in the middle of the river, Flapjack was making mud balls and cakes on the riverbank. Mattie sighed. Flapjack was enjoying playtime while the other beavers worked.

Mattie looked at the sky. A storm was coming in. Lots of rain, then a flood. If the dam wasn't finished soon, the high water would wash away all the work they'd done.

From the river's edge, Mattie watched as several beavers swam from the dam in the middle of the river to collect mud from the riverbank. They carried mud cupped in their tails to the dam, where other beavers used it to plug holes and cracks between the logs. Swimming back and forth between the dam and the riverbank was hard work, not to mention a poor use of time. Mattie had an idea.

"Hey, Flapjack," said Mattie. "Can you throw that mud ball with your tail and hit the dam out in the middle of the river?"

"Sure," replied Flapjack. "I mean, I guess so."

"Well, give it a try," said Mattie.

Flapjack cupped a mud ball into his tail. He gazed out at the dam in the middle of the river, and sized up the distance from the riverbank to the dam. Everyone was watching. They started to cheer. "Come on, Flapjack. You can do it."

"Hummph!" grunted Flapjack, as he hurled the mud ball with his tail. It sailed high into the air. And landed . . . smack! . . . in the middle of the river. Flapjack had missed.

"Ahhhh!" said the crowd in disappointment.

"Wait, everyone," said Flapjack, as he gathered up another mud ball with his tail. Flapjack gritted his teeth. He stared a long time at his target. Then he gave it all he had. *Hummph!* His tail acted like a catapult. *Whish* went the mud ball as he launched it from his tail. *Splat!* The mud ball landed smack in the middle of the dam.

Everyone cheered. The beavers rushed to the dam. They wheeled around, and used their tails to pat the mud down into the cracks of the logs. Waddles broke into a grin. "Do it again," he shouted.

Flapjack did. He threw another mud ball right in the middle of the dam. Bull's eye. The beavers patted it into the cracks. "Again!" they yelled.

All day long, Flapjack threw mud ball after mud ball. The other beavers didn't have to swim back and forth between the dam and the riverbank. They just stayed on the dam catching Flapjack's mud balls and plastering them into the dam.

This saved the beavers time and energy. They finished building their dam just in the nick of time. That night the rains came. It rained hard for hours. The river soon flooded, covering the surrounding fields and woods in water.

All the animals of the river valley were soaking wet and miserable. All except the beavers. They holed up in a warm, comfy den inside their dam. Waddles was the first to speak. "Thanks Mattie and Flapjack. If it weren't for you, we never would've finished the dam before the rains came."

Mattie said, "It was only right that Flapjack helped. But it was also good that we let him contribute in his own special way. Isn't that right, Flapjack?"

Mattie and the other beavers heard only snores. Flapjack was fast asleep. He was worn out, but very happy, from a hard day's play.

30

The Royal Bulldog

Author's Note: Family pets offer a limitless source of ideas for stories. Children easily relate to made-up adventures about their pets because they are so familiar with the personalities and habits of their own dogs, cats, birds, or hamsters. Our family bulldog, Spencer, was famous among relatives and friends for being the most pampered dog in the world. It required no stretch of the imagination to create the following story about a princely dog born into a life of luxury.

ONCE UPON A TIME, there lived in India a great Maharajah (that's sort of like a prince) who lived in a golden palace. The Maharajah had many valuable possessions—jewels, gold, fine clothes—but there was one possession he prized above all others. It was his pet bulldog, Raja. Raja had been a gift of the British Viceroy (that's like a governor), who lived in the capital of Delhi, not far away.

Raja had the finest foods to eat, plenty of play toys, and slept on a large, satin pillow. He wore a collar with his name spelled out in diamonds. He had attendants who fanned him when it got too hot. Raja was so pampered that the Maharajah's subjects referred to him as the Royal Bulldog. Raja was very lazy. In fact, sleeping was his favorite thing to do. It was easy to be lazy when the Maharajah's servants waited on you all day.

One day, an awful tragedy fell upon the Maharajah's kingdom. The neighboring king started a war against the Maharajah and his subjects. Many people died, and the Maharajah and most of his subjects were forced to flee their kingdom.

The Maharajah was in such a hurry to run away that he forgot to take Raja with him. In fact, Raja slept through most of the fighting. He slept so soundly and quietly that no one even noticed him.

The day after the fighting stopped, Raja woke up from his long nap. He was very surprised to find everyone gone. Where was his kingly breakfast? His golden water bowl?

His morning back rub? He was very hungry and thirsty. But most of all, he missed the companionship of the Maharajah and his servants.

Raja walked through the palace looking for food and companionship. The palace was empty and silent. He sniffed around the royal bedrooms, but the Maharajah's scent had grown cold. All the things that made the palace his home were gone.

Raja left the palace and wandered down one of the roads leading out of town. Raja had never been out of the palace before. The Maharajah had always wanted to keep Raja safe and sheltered inside the palace complex. Until then, Raja had never before seen sick people and animals. He had never experienced any type of unkindness or cruelty. Now he saw the world as it really was, and it made him sad.

Raja walked slowly down to the river. He saw a small boy named Siddharth, playing happily by the riverbank. Siddharth was laughing and dancing. He was the first person Raja had seen smiling the entire day. For the first time in days, Raja felt happy. Wagging his stump tail, he ran toward Siddharth.

Suddenly, Raja heard a big crash. He saw, to his horror, a huge crocodile jump out of the water. The crocodile snapped its jaws at Siddharth. Siddharth jumped out of the way as the crocodile's jaws slammed shut just inches away from his body. Unfortunately for Siddharth, the crocodile's scraggly teeth hooked his clothing. Siddharth couldn't get away. The crocodile's eyes gleamed. He still had his prize on the hook. The crocodile began to slink back into the water, pulling Siddharth with him.

Raja's heart ached for Siddharth. Raja realized he had to do something. If he didn't, the crocodile would drag Siddharth under the bubbling water and drown him. Luckily for Siddharth, Raja had one strength that few other dogs can rival. Bulldogs have very, very strong jaws. Raja crouched into a low stance. He leapt at the crocodile. Raja's jaws clamped down on the crocodile's snout. Instantly, Siddharth's clothing tore free. The crocodile thrashed around in pain and confusion, taking Raja for a wild ride. But Raja held on. Finally, the crocodile grew still. He emitted a barely audible rumble from his throat. Raja released his grip. Once Raja let the crocodile go, the crocodile slid back into the water, never to be seen again.

Many villagers who heard the commotion came running to help. They saw Raja's fight with the crocodile and how he had saved Siddharth. They surrounded Raja, showering him with pets and caresses. Then Siddharth wrapped his arms around Raja's neck and gave him a big hug. "Come home with me. You can live with my family."

Raja followed Siddharth home. Siddharth gave Raja his first proper meal in days. Siddharth and his family took good care of Raja. Though Raja got no more backrubs,

Siddharth played fetch with him every day. While Raja didn't eat rich foods in a golden bowl, the family shared whatever they had to eat with him. Better than a satin pillow, Raja got to sleep by Siddharth every night. Though Raja was no longer a Royal Bulldog, he was much happier in his new life—as just a regular dog.

The Fruit Bat and the Vampire Bat

Author's Note: When parents and children create stories together, they can never anticipate some of the wild, far out, and fun characters they'll come up with. Here's an example.

IN THE RAIN forests of Central America, there lived a vampire bat and a fruit bat. Even though they were both bats, they didn't have much in common. Fruit Bat, of course, liked to eat fruit from the jungle trees, especially the mango trees. His favorite meal was eating mangoes after they had gotten a little too ripe in the jungle sun. Mmmm . . . there's no better food in the world than rotting fruit on the vine!

Vampire Bat didn't agree. "Yuck," he said. "Who wants to eat rotting fruit? It's all slimy and smelly and covered with flies!" Vampire bats prefer to eat something else. "Blood!" said Vampire Bat. Just the sound of the word made his eyes brighten. "There's nothing better than to lick up the warm, sweet-smelling drops of blood oozing from fresh bite marks."

"That's disgusting," said Fruit Bat. His face contorted into a grimace. "I don't understand why any bat has to bite another animal to get its food."

"I don't hurt the animals I bite," said Vampire Bat, slightly upset. "I lightly puncture the animal's skin and lap up about a spoonful of blood. My stomach doesn't hold that much anyway. Besides, the animals I bite rarely feel a thing. I usually do my feeding at night. The animals sleep right through it."

"But don't you like to bite humans in the neck and suck their blood?" asked Fruit Bat.

"That's just an old fairy tale to scare human kids," explained Vampire Bat. "I usually only bite cows. Cows are my favorite." Vampire Bat licked his lips.

"But cows are some of my best friends," protested Fruit Bat.

"I'm telling you, the cows never feel a thing," said Vampire Bat. "Besides, have one of your cow friends ever complained to you about vampire bats?"

"I guess not," said Fruit Bat.

"Well, there you go," said Vampire Bat. "Now if you'll excuse me, I've got some cows to see." And off Vampire Bat flew.

Fruit Bat still wasn't convinced. "I like cows, and I don't like the idea of creepy little vampire bats biting them and sucking their blood. Maybe there's something I can do to warn the cows!"

Off he flew to a nearby cattle ranch where Vampire Bat liked to visit. Fruit Bat flew into the barn through a hole in the roof. He found the leader of the herd, a black and white cow named Luisa.

"Luisa," said Fruit Bat. "Did you know that Vampire Bat is sneaking into your barn at night? He bites you and the other cows in the neck."

"What?" asked Luisa. Her eyes grew as big as saucers.

"And that's not the worst part. He sucks your blood for dinner."

Luisa was shocked. "Are you sure?"

"I'm sure."

By this time the other cows had gathered around Luisa and heard the story. "We had no idea," said another cow, a big white and tan named Pablo.

"It's true," said Fruit Bat. "Most of the time you sleep through the night and never know Vampire Bat has feasted on your blood."

"What can we do to stop him?" asked Luisa.

"I have an idea," replied Fruit Bat. "Keep one cow awake through the night to shoo away Vampire Bat when he tries to come for a meal. You can take turns."

"How will we know when he comes?" asked Pablo.

"Keep your eyes on that hole." Fruit Bat pointed a fingered wing toward the roof. "I bet he'll come in the barn the same way I did."

That night the cows tried Fruit Bat's plan. One stayed awake for a two-hour watch. When that cow's watch was done, she woke up another cow to take the next shift.

Around midnight, Luisa took her turn on duty. Before long she saw in the moonlight a black shape flutter into the barn through the hole in the roof. Luisa watched carefully. It was Vampire Bat. He dove and fixed himself on Pablo's neck. "Caught you," said Luisa. She woke the other cows with a low, mournful "MooOOOO!"

"What's going on?" said a sleepy Pablo.

"Vampire Bat is on your neck," said Luisa. "Shake him off!"

Pablo shook his head and neck back and forth. A dizzy Vampire Bat finally let go and flew up to the rafters.

"What gives?" cried Vampire Bat. "You never complained when I did this before."

"We never knew before that you were drinking our blood," said Luisa.

"How did you find out?" asked Vampire Bat.

Tina, another cow who wasn't the herd's smartest, blurted out, "It was Fruit B. . .,"

"Shhh!" interrupted Luisa. "Don't give away our source!"

"What did you say?" asked Vampire Bat. "Fruit . . . what?"

"Never mind," said Tina.

"Oh, I know," exclaimed Vampire Bat. "It must've been Fruit Bat who warned you. I should've known. He and I never get along."

"What are you going to do to Fruit Bat?" asked Tina.

The question woke Vampire Bat up from his thoughts. "Oh, you'll see," said Vampire Bat.

The next night, Vampire Bat and a few of his friends went on a fruit tree rampage. The vampire bats knocked every piece of fruit down from all the trees in Fruit Bat's neighborhood. Most of the fruit that fell to the ground was quickly eaten by the jungle floor dwellers, especially the capybaras. The monkeys, birds, and insects gobbled up the rest. It was quite a bountiful feast for all the animals of the jungle, save one . . . Fruit Bat. He was the only animal left out.

The following days were tough ones for both bats. All the fruit trees in the area had been stripped of their fruit, so Fruit Bat had nothing to eat. The same was true for Vampire Bat. Word spread among the nearby cattle barns that Vampire Bat liked to drink cows' blood. All the cows learned to keep sentries on duty to shoo away Vampire Bat. All those cows, but not one drop of blood to drink!

"It's all your fault," said Fruit Bat. "We wouldn't be starving if it weren't for you!"

"Me?" exclaimed Vampire Bat. "You're the one who ruined things for me in the cattle barns. I can't go for more than a couple of days without blood to eat, or I'll die."

The two argued for quite a while, until both went silent. The two remained quiet for a long time.

Finally, Fruit Bat spoke up. "If we don't learn to get along we're both going to starve to death. And that wouldn't solve anything."

"I agree," replied Vampire Bat.

Fruit Bat continued, "We don't have to like each other to get along, do we?"

"No," said Vampire Bat. "We're just different. That's all there is to it."

The two stayed silent for several more minutes.

"Promise you won't wreck any more fruit trees?" asked Fruit Bat. "There are more trees upriver. I'll have to fly a long way to get to them, but at least I'll have something to eat."

"I won't," said Vampire Bat, "if you promise not to warn the cows on the ranches across the river. I'll just have to fly a little longer to get to them."

"I promise," said Fruit Bat.

From that day on, Fruit Bat and Vampire Bat learned to get along, despite their differences. Fruit Bat even got Vampire Bat to eat a little fruit. At first, Vampire Bat didn't want to. But when Fruit Bat said they were going to eat blood oranges, Vampire Bat couldn't resist, saying, "Well, in that case, they can't be all bad!"

One Little Katydid

Author's Note: Storytelling is always more fun when you can tell a bedtime story to a group of kids. Some of our closest friends, who have a family with four children, often spend part of their summer vacation visiting us at the beach. At the end of a fun day, the kids always want a bedtime story. During our storytelling, they sometimes get a little silly. There are times when I think they never listen to a word I say. But there are other times— when I'm really on a roll with a story—that I'll look into their eyes and see that I have each of them mesmerized. There's no better feeling than to know you might be creating a special childhood memory for your children or their friends. Years afterwards, much to my astonishment, our kids still remember all the best stories I told them on those summer nights during vacation.

During one summer evening story, I began, as usual, by asking the kids what they wanted their story to be about. One of our friends' daughters, Katie, asked for a story about a little girl named Katie. Here's the story I came up with on the spur of the moment, about a little female katydid named—what else—Katie.

ONCE UPON A TIME, there was a family of katydids who lived on a huge, green lawn. Theirs wasn't the only family of katydids who lived on the lawn. In fact, there were thousands of other katydid families who shared the same lawn for eating, sleeping, sunning, and generally having a good time.

Life was indeed pleasant for the katydids. They had plenty of grass to eat and very few enemies that tried to eat them. The lawn sprinklers came on once a day and gave them plenty to drink, along with a nice bath. On the whole, every day was a good day.

Except Wednesdays. Wednesday was mowing day. On Wednesday, gardeners came to cut the grass with their big, fast, powerful mowers. Nothing terrified the katydids more than a power mower coughing to life. Vrooom! Vroooooom! VROOOMMMM!!!!

The mowers especially scared the youngest daughter in the katydid family. Her name was Katie. (Katie was a most popular name for baby girl katydids.) What terrified Katie most were the whirling blades of the mower that sliced every insect in their path into microscopic bug clippings. The katydids had to hop for their lives every time the lawn mowers appeared.

The mowers so terrified Katie that her parents called a meeting of all the katydid families to discuss what could be done. The meeting was held between the double rows of boxwoods enclosing their lawn. There the katydids argued what to do. Many wanted to sabotage the mowers. Some suggested they chew holes into the mower's gas lines. But others argued that katydids were too little and weak to tamper with mower engines.

Little Katie despaired of hearing what the katydids couldn't do. "You're right," she said to the leaders of the katydid council. "Each of us alone is too small and weak to do anything about the mowers . . ."

A katydid elder interrupted. "That's just what we were saying."

"Please let me finish," Katie pleaded. "While each of us is too small and weak on her own, if we all worked together, we could get rid of those nasty lawn mowers."

"How are we going to do that?" said another katydid. "Lawn mowers are machines. We're just frail little insects."

Katie smiled. "Lawn mowers may be machines, but we have strength in numbers. Listen to me. I have a plan." She told everyone about her plan. To Katie's surprise, the other katydids liked it. Everyone decided that the following Wednesday would be the day when the katydids fought back.

The next Wednesday began just like every other Wednesday. Early in the morning, the gardeners started their power mowers. They drove them onto the katydids' lawn. But instead of panicking, not one katydid could be seen hopping about the lawn. Everyone was unusually calm.

Calm, that is, until Katie gave the order. Just as the gardeners set to work, tens of thousands of katydids swarmed out of the hedges surrounding the lawn. They fell upon the gardeners and their mowers. Every katydid on the lawn took part. But not just the katydids living on the lawn. Katie had sent out word to all the neighboring lawns, fields, and forests. She asked all katydids living nearby to come and help.

And help they did. The katydids swarmed the gardeners. The gardeners swatted at them with their caps. The katydids tormented them so much that the gardeners jumped off their mowers and ran away. The katydids didn't relent. They chased the gardeners for nearly a mile down the road. So terrifying was the experience that the gardeners never returned to work.

The lawn mowers themselves fared worse. The katydids chewed up all their wires and fuel lines. None worked again.

Katie was a hero. She alone recognized what could be accomplished when everyone worked together. And the lawn never even needed mowing again. The katydids *(munch, munch!)* made sure the grass was trimmed neatly every day.

ADVENTURES AND
FOLK TALES

A Mariner's Good Fortune

Author's Note: Kids love a good adventure story. Adventures seem to be the stories that stay with children the longest. When I asked my oldest son why he loved adventure stories so much, he said it was because adventures combined all the best parts of other stories: myths, legends, action, suspense, danger, quests, sci-fi, and (for girls) romance. Kids are also drawn to the super-sized heroes or villains in adventure stories. Nothing captures a child's imagination more than tales about outlaws, daredevils, sleuths, genies, wizards, gamblers, knights, pirates or, as in the story below, a dashing swashbuckler.

ONCE UPON A TIME, THERE WAS A SEA GODDESS named Kalliste. She was a very moody goddess. When she was happy, the skies were clear and the seas calm. Perfect weather for sailing. But when she was mad, storm clouds gathered. The wind blew stronger, and the ocean became rough. When Kalliste grew angry, that was the time for all sailors to beware.

Now, there was also a great ship's captain named Bartholomew. His friends simply called him Captain Bart. Captain Bart was the greatest sailor in the world. He had sailed on every ocean and sea, and in every type of weather, even in the worst storms imaginable. His crew had complete trust in him and called him Lucky Bart.

One day, Captain Bart and his crew set sail from England to China by way of Cape Horn, the southernmost tip of South America. Some of the roughest seas in the world can be found around Cape Horn. The crew wasn't afraid, because they had Lucky Bart as their captain.

The weather on the first leg of their voyage to Cape Horn bode well for Captain Bart and his crew. The sun shown, and there was a stiff breeze to fill their sails. The crew was in good spirits. But Captain Bart was anxious. Before leaving England, he lost his lucky charm. It was a miniature ship's anchor made of real gold, which he wore around his neck. The first captain under whom Bart served as first mate had given him the lucky charm. It always brought him luck, and had saved him on many a perilous voyage. His lucky charm was the real reason behind why his crew called him Lucky Bart.

What made Captain Bart even more anxious was how he lost his lucky charm. On his last night in England, Captain Bart played cards. After gambling away all his money, he bet his gold ship's anchor in one last, desperate attempt to win his money back. And lost it. Captain Bart knew he had tempted fate and prepared himself for the worst.

Sure enough, the weather did become worse. Much worse. As they neared the Cape, a great storm arose. The winds and sea grew rough and threatening. This wasn't an ordinary storm. It was a hurricane, moving in a giant circle hundreds of miles wide. Strong winds and driving rain dashed the ship. With each great wave that the ship climbed and descended, the crew became more and more scared.

When the storm was at its worst, a mist collected over the waves next to the ship. The mist started spinning like a tornado. Then it stopped to form the face and body of a beautiful woman. Kalliste.

"So, Captain Bart," said Kalliste, "it appears you've tempted fate one too many times."

Captain Bart, standing at the helm of his ship, replied defiantly, "What is it that you want of me, you crafty sea witch?" Inside, Captain Bart wasn't so confident. He prayed that Kalliste didn't know about his lost charm.

"My, my, my," said Kalliste. "You're mighty plucky for being in the middle of such a violent storm."

"I've seen worse," called Captain Bart. "Say what you want of me, or be gone."

Kalliste smiled. "I want your ship, and the lives of you and your crew. It's time to pay an old gambling debt."

Captain Bart didn't like the sound of that. Did Kalliste know he had gambled away his lucky charm? Despite his doubts, Captain Bart spoke in a confident voice. "You cannot sink our ship. I've weathered far worse storms than this."

"Not without your lucky charm," said Kalliste with a sly grin.

Captain Bart's worst fears had come true.

Kalliste rose in the mist. "Oh, yes. I know all about your lucky charm. I know that your first captain gave it to you. And that his first captain had given it to him. I know, for a fact, that this lucky charm has been passed from captain to first mate for over seven generations."

"How could you possibly know that?" asked Captain Bart, much less confident now.

"Because I'm the one who gave the lucky charm to the very first sea captain long, long ago." Kalliste's angry face and voice softened for a moment. "His name was Captain Swan. I was madly in love with him. I gave the charm magical powers to protect its wearer from sea and storm. I never wanted Captain Swan to come to any harm."

The anger in Kalliste's voice returned. "But he, like you, didn't appreciate my gift. We got into a lover's quarrel, and Swan gave my gift to his first mate. And when his first mate became a captain, he gave it to his first mate. And so on, until it came to you." Captain Bart realized for the first time how his lucky charm had come to be.

"Until you lost it in a card game the night before you set sail!" shrieked Kalliste. Kalliste pointed her finger at Bart's face. "The only thing that can save you from this storm is your lucky charm. Yet you carelessly lost it playing cards."

Captain Bart was stunned. Kalliste did know, after all, how he lost his lucky charm. But Captain Bart decided to try and bluff his way out of this predicament.

"I only lost it temporarily," he yelled. "The man I lost it to promised he would hold it for me until I bought it back from him, at double the cost. I'm on my way now to China with a hold filled with cargo. I expect to make enough money to buy back my lucky charm when I return to England."

"Very clever," said Kalliste. "But I also know for a fact that this man has no intention of selling it back to you."

Captain Bart didn't like the sound of that. "How do you know that?"

"Because it was I who dressed up as a man your last night in port. It was I who won your lucky charm in that card game." Kalliste unfolded her hands and held before Captain Bart the ship's anchor he had gambled away. "Without this," she said, "you're doomed."

Two times now, Kalliste had caught Captain Bart by surprise. But he wasn't about to be surprised a third time. He had to think fast. "Come on, Lucky Bart," he said to himself, "keep your wits about you."

"Double or nothing," he blurted out.

"What do you mean, double or nothing?" Kalliste hesitated.

"I mean to wage another bet with you," said Captain Bart. "If I win, I get the lucky charm back. And my ship is saved."

"And if you lose?"

"You get my crew, my ship, and . . . ," Captain Bart paused.

Kalliste slithered up next to Captain Bart and whispered in his ear. "And what?"

"My soul," said Captain Bart. "I'll be your loyal servant for all eternity, to make amends for Captain Swan's disloyalty those many years ago."

Kalliste stretched her arms and purred. "That's a very tempting offer. But what's the wager?"

Again, Captain Bart had to think fast. "You're not the only one here who understands the weather and the seas. Even without my lucky charm, I'll wager you that within the hour, the winds will die down and the seas will calm."

"That's impossible. I'm the goddess of the sea!" Kalliste's voice rose. "Only I can control the seas."

"Do we have a bet or not?" shouted Captain Bart.

"You're on," said Kalliste. "I'll return in one hour. If the seas and the weather haven't calmed, then everything is mine. Your crew. Your ship. Your life. And your soul!"

In a flash, Kalliste's form disappeared into the mists.

The crew was terrified. "Can you really calm the seas?" they asked.

"They don't call me Lucky Bart for nothing," said Captain Bart. He spoke in a commanding voice to give them courage. Inwardly, he wasn't so sure.

The crew stared at the ship's hourglass, marking the time. Fifteen minutes passed. Then a half hour. Nothing changed. When the sand in the glass ran out at the end of an hour, the crew gasped and looked around them. If anything, the storm seemed worse.

Without warning, a cloud of mist gathered and swirled around the captain's deck. "Time's up," said Kalliste, appearing from the mist. "Begging for mercy now will do you no good. A bet is a bet."

Captain Bart appeared calm and assured. "Hold on one moment, old girl. My luck needs just one more minute to work its magic."

"A thousand minutes won't help you now," said Kalliste. "Prepare yourselves for your fate."

With an upward motion of her hand, Kalliste lifted a giant tidal wave from the stormy ocean. But before she could send it crashing upon the ship, a ray of sunlight broke through the clouds upon her face.

Kalliste looked up. "What's this? A ray of sunlight in the midst of a storm?"

In the next instant, the clouds began to clear, and the seas calmed. Soon, the sun shone. There wasn't a cloud above them now. The only dark clouds that could be seen were scattered on the horizon.

"It's a miracle," shouted the crew. "How can this be?"

Suddenly, Kalliste realized what had happened. She briefly forgot what type of storm she had created to sink Captain Bart's ship.

Captain Bart shook his fist at Kalliste. "That's right, Kalliste. You forgot you made a hurricane. And what does every hurricane have?"

Kalliste crossed her arms and sighed. "An eye."

"We don't understand," said the crew to their captain.

"Don't you see, men," said Captain Bart. "All hurricanes swirl around in a great, big circle. In the middle of the circle, there's a calm center called the eye. Even though the outside of the swirling circle is filled with ferocious seas and winds, the eye is always calm, with the sun shining above placid waters. Isn't that right, Kalliste?"

"Yes," said Kalliste. Her teeth clenched in anger.

Captain Bart turned back to his men. "I was counting on the fact that Kalliste forgot she had created not just any old storm, but a hurricane, the most dangerous storm there is. I knew that the eye of the hurricane was fast approaching. That's why I bet Kalliste that the seas and winds would calm within the hour. I never said I'd be the one to calm them. Now pay up your bet, Kalliste!"

"It's not fair!" screamed Kalliste.

"Fair or not," said Captain Bart, "a bet is a bet. Isn't that what you once said?"

Kalliste's red face was boiling with anger. But when she realized how clever Captain Bart had been, she allowed a sliver of a smile to cross her face. "You won this time," she said. "But don't forget you still have to sail your ship through the outer wall of the hurricane."

"Not a problem," said Captain Bart. "As long as I have my lucky charm, my crew and I can sail through anything. Speaking of my lucky charm . . ."

"Very well," said Kalliste, "here it is." She handed the golden ship's anchor to Captain Bart. In a tornado of movement, she disappeared into the mist.

Captain Bart kissed the lucky charm and placed it once again around his neck. "Come on men," he shouted. "Man your stations. We still have to sail our way back through the other end of this hurricane."

The men had new life and jumped to their stations. Though the voyage through the back end of the hurricane was treacherous, they managed to pop through the hurricane wall in safety. In a few hours, the hurricane was well behind them, and the sun appeared.

"Three cheers for Lucky Bart!" shouted his crew. "Huzzah! Huzzah! HUZZAH!"

Captain Bart smiled. He felt for his lucky charm and was reassured to find it safely around his neck. "I promise I'll be more careful with you from now on," he said quietly to himself.

"You had better be," whispered a voice off to starboard. Captain Bart wheeled to his right and saw Kalliste hovering above the water. "Because if you're careless again, I'll be there to snatch it from you."

"Be gone, Kalliste," said Captain Bart. "Leave me be. I've learned my lesson once and for all." And he kissed his charm one more time. For luck.

The Phoenix and the Volcano of Gold

Author's Note: Sometimes, when you're telling a story to a group of kids, they can't agree on what they want their story to be about. If that happens, choosing one child's story idea over another may cause a riot. To preserve bedtime peace and quiet, try having each child pick one object, person, or animal to be included in the story. Then combine the different subjects into one story. In our home, we call these combination stories.

For example, I asked my sons to come up with four objects, persons, or animals to combine into a story. I knew that I really had to put on my thinking cap when they came up with (1) a phoenix, (2) a tooth, (3) a treasure of gold, and (4) a mountain. Yikes! What on earth do those four objects have in common? Using a bit of poetic license (a volcano is actually a mountain, after all, and there is nothing in mythology that says a phoenix can't have teeth), here is the story I came up with.

LONG AGO, YOUNG KNIGHTS SOUGHT TO PROVE THEIR BRAVERY and worth by undertaking a quest. A quest was a sort of adventure, whereby a knight might try to save a maiden in distress, or rid the kingdom of an ogre or dragon. Should the knight prevail in his quest, the king rewarded him by offering his daughter's hand in marriage, or perhaps a bag of gold. Only knights were worthy enough to go on quests. Commoners were thought to lack the necessary bravery and skill in battle.

One day, the King summoned his knights and gave them a challenge. "Young knights!" shouted the King. "I've been told by a wizard traveling through my kingdom that there's a treasure of gold waiting to be captured in the high mountains bordering our kingdom. Among the tallest of those mountains you'll find a fiery volcano, in whose depths the earth's fire has forged rocks and boulders made of pure gold. The gold is just lying about the volcano's crater, waiting only for a brave knight to seize it for his king and kingdom. Who among you is brave enough to undertake this quest?"

All the knights shouted that they were ready to accept the King's challenge. The King commanded them to be quiet with a gesture of his hand. "Only the most worthy of knights may win the gold," he said. "It's guarded by a phoenix—one of the mystical firebirds of old. Only a knight skilled with the sword, mace, or bow may slay the phoenix, because it possesses many deadly weapons. Not only does it have sharp teeth and claws, but it breathes fire and spits poison. The wizard has warned that no knight has ever survived a meeting with the phoenix."

The King's warning did nothing to quench the enthusiasm of the knights for this quest. One by one, they slowly made their way into the high mountains. One by one, they scaled the fiery volcano to meet their fate. The legend proved true enough. In the crater formed at the top of the volcano were strewn rocks of all sizes. All made of pure gold! But the gold was indeed guarded by one of the fiercest creatures the knights had ever seen. The phoenix was the size of a castle tower, with claws and teeth as long as a man's body. Its weapons were deadlier than even the King had warned. Not only could the phoenix breathe fire and spit poison, but its very gaze could turn a knight into a pillar of stone should he look directly into the phoenix's fiery eyes.

One by one the knights drew their swords, or swung their maces, or loosed their arrows upon the phoenix. And one by one the knights were slain by the phoenix right where they stood. The lucky ones were those who were turned into stone after looking into the phoenix's deadly stare. The unlucky ones were those who were burned to a crisp from the dragon's breath, or were poisoned by the venom the phoenix spat upon their faces and bodies.

The King despaired greatly when none of his knights returned from their quests. It was he, after all, who had sent them forth, and he felt personally responsible. A terrible sadness descended upon the King. Could no one slay the terrible phoenix that had killed so many brave knights?

Meanwhile, the common folk of the kingdom had their own problems. Many of the peasants couldn't grow enough food to feed their families or make enough money to pay the rent. Two brothers, Richard and John, had just lost their father and now faced starvation because their land was too poor and rocky to grow food. With no food to eat or sell at market, they soon fell behind on the rent money they owed their landlord. The landlord wasn't sympathetic.

"You have one week to pay your back rent, or I'll have the county sheriff throw you off my land."

"But sir," begged Richard, "how can we possibly make enough money in just a week's time to pay off our rent?"

"For all I care," said the landlord, "you could do what so many knights have attempted and failed. Slay the phoenix of the volcano and bring back the gold it guards. However you get it, I want the rent paid in full in one week. Or else."

"And if we die trying?" said Richard.

"Then I won't have to go to the trouble of evicting you from my land!" said the landlord.

As the landlord rode away, John looked at Richard and said, "You heard the landlord. Let's go to the volcano and bring back the gold. It's the only way to keep our home."

"But how can we do what noble knights could not?" pleaded Richard. "We're farmers, not fighters. We're no match for that phoenix."

"But we need the money," said John. "Besides, we're as worthy as the next man." Richard ultimately agreed with John to venture to the volcano to seek the gold. He could think of no other, safer way to find the money to pay their landlord.

The next day, the two brothers began their long journey to the volcano. They carried just a few provisions, and for protection, only their hunting knives and bows. As the two brothers approached the volcano, they spoke of their father. The brothers loved their father and missed him greatly. Would he have approved of this journey? What would he have told them to do when they finally faced the phoenix?

Despite their bedraggled, un-knightly appearance, they did have one thing in their favor. They were excellent archers and superb hunters. Their father had taught them well.

The climb to the rim of the volcano was steep and arduous. The brothers had to use their hands to pull themselves up the last few feet. The rotten-egg stink of the sulphur burning within the volcano made the boys cringe. When they finally stood up on the rim of the volcano, they were both awestruck and terrified by what they saw.

There in the middle of the crater was a pool of bubbling, red lava. Strewn around the crater floor were hundreds, perhaps thousands, of golden boulders and rocks. Even the sand on the crater floor looked to be made of gold dust. Every now and then, the lava pool belched out a huge golden rock onto the crater floor. The volcano was an active blast furnace, forging rocks of gold deep within its bowels.

But the sight that caused their knees to shake and their palms to sweat was the huge firebird sleeping by the shore of the lava pool. The phoenix was enormous, with long steely claws and scales pulsating red and black like burning lava. As the brothers watched, the phoenix stretched and yawned, revealing a beaked mouth full of rows of jagged teeth.

"This is our chance," said John to his brother. "Let's shoot him before he discovers us."

"I suppose," said Richard, not convinced.

"Aim for his heart," said John.

"Why his heart?" asked Richard. "Why not between his eyes?"

"I don't know. I once heard that's the only way to kill dragons."

"But this is a phoenix," cried Richard.

"Does it really matter?" said John. "Let's stop arguing before the phoenix discovers us."

Both brothers pulled arrows from their quivers. They fitted them to their bowstrings. Their father taught his sons how to make their own arrows. The ones they chose were especially long, made to fly straight and true. John and Richard drew their bows back, aimed at the phoenix's heart, and . . .

Did nothing. Both began to shake with the thought that if they missed, the phoenix would discover their presence and kill them. The magnitude of what they were about to do suddenly drained them of their courage.

"Why don't you shoot?" asked John, still holding his drawn bow.

"Why don't you shoot?" replied Richard, sweat pouring down his face.

"Because I'm as scared as you," John said.

Richard wiped the sweat from this brow. "What are we going to do?"

"I don't know," said John. "What would father tell us to do right now?"

Richard thought for a moment. "He would tell us to use his old bow hunting trick. Aim at your target, then close your eyes and only release your arrow when you can feel your shot."

"It's worth a try," said John. The thought of their father and his lessons restored the brothers' courage. Both turned back to their target with new confidence.

To their dismay, the brothers discovered that the phoenix now was not only awake, but had spotted them standing on the crater's edge. The brothers took so long gathering their courage and deciding what to do that they had lost the element of surprise.

The phoenix shrieked and spread its wings to take flight. The noise from the phoenix sounded like a hundred hawks screeching at once.

"It's now or never," shouted Richard over the din. "Do what father taught us."

John shouted his father's command. "Aim at its heart. Close your eyes. Fire when you feel the shot."

Having hunted together for so long, the brothers fired their arrows at the exact same instant. Their arrows found their mark and both entered the phoenix's heart at once. Blood poured from its chest, and the huge beast's legs buckled from the mortal wound.

"We did it," shouted the amazed brothers. They watched the phoenix topple dead to the ground.

But their joy quickly turned to dread. As the phoenix's head hit the rocky ground, its teeth shattered into dozens of jagged shards. The shards were the seeds of a new generation. They quickly transformed and grew into dozens of baby phoenixes.

Luckily for the brothers, these infant phoenixes were too young to have yet developed poison or a fiery breath. But they still had sharp claws and teeth. They turned their anger at the brothers for having killed their parent. The infants spread their wings, took flight, and dive-bombed Richard and John. They bit at their faces and tried to peck out their eyes.

"What do we do now?" shouted Richard to John, trying to make himself heard over the frenzy.

"Shoot your arrows as fast as you can," John yelled. The two brothers fired off twenty arrows at the phoenixes in as many seconds.

Unfortunately for the brothers, the infant phoenixes proved too agile to be hit in the air. The brothers used up their quivers without hitting a single phoenix.

"We have no more weapons," shouted Richard. "We're done for."

"Never give up," screamed John, as a phoenix banked by his head. "Throw rocks at them if you have to."

Desperation gripped the brothers. Mustering every ounce of strength they had left, the brothers picked up as many rocks as they could and hurled them at the phoenixes. Though they didn't come close to hitting any, a miraculous thing happened. The parent phoenix had been bred to guard the volcano's gold, and its offspring had inherited this trait. When the brothers threw their golden rocks into the air or down the mountainside, the infants stopped attacking the brothers and chased after the rocks instead. Like dogs fetching balls, the phoenixes brought back the golden rocks the brothers had thrown and placed them for safekeeping in a cache by the lava pool.

Soon, the brothers became amused by their newly discovered power. "Go fetch, you silly birds," yelled John, as he tossed a rock of gold down the mountainside. Three phoenixes immediately jumped over the side of the volcano to fetch it. Richard then tossed a large nugget of gold straight up into the air, causing two to collide in mid-air as they both tried to catch it. "Serves you right," said Richard in amusement.

With the phoenixes distracted, the brothers took the opportunity to stuff their pockets and knapsacks full of gold. "Quick now," said Richard, "let's get out of here while these birds are busy chasing after the gold rocks we've thrown."

The boys ran down the slope of the volcano, thinking that they had made good on their escape. But the volcano wouldn't give up its treasures so easily. As the parent phoenix lay dead in the volcano's crater, the blood from its heart slowly streamed along the ground toward the lava pool. As soon as the blood dripped into the lava pool, tremors began to convulse the volcano. While the volcano may have lost its guardian phoenix and some of its gold, it wasn't going to let those responsible escape. It gathered steam to erupt.

The volcano shook. "Run for it," yelled John. The brothers scampered down the volcano's slope. Molten rocks dropped around them. "Quick," shouted John. "Make for the river!"

At the base of the volcano, a small river flowed along the edge of the surrounding forest. Its source was in the high mountains above, and near the base of the volcano it dropped off in a waterfall to the valley below. As the volcano's lava and burning rocks nipped at the brothers' heels, the brothers dove headlong into the river. They swam underwater while the volcano exploded above them, showering down fire and ash.

As the world around them burst into flame, the brothers came up for one more breath. They grasped each other's hands, and then let the river carry them over the waterfall. Though it was only a few seconds, they dropped through space for what seemed like many minutes. Their sickened stomachs cried out for the free fall to stop. They splashed into the pool below, and were dragged underneath the water's foam by the force of the pool's currents and by the weight of the gold in their pockets.

Gathering their remaining strength, the brothers surged toward the surface. Their lungs were pinched and screaming for air. The brothers popped through the swirling currents above and filled their lungs with cool, fresh air. They had made it! They slowly paddled over to the edge of the pool, pulled themselves out of the water and collapsed on the bank. The brothers were so exhausted that they lay on the sandy bank of the pool for almost an hour, unable to move.

When at last their strength returned, Richard and John quickly and happily set off for home. As they put distance between themselves and the volcano, the volcano seemed to realize that further belching and erupting would do it no good, and slowly quieted down.

The brothers returned to their home and took stock of the gold they had taken from the volcano's crater. Their stash was much greater than they thought. They realized that not only were they rich, they were probably, outside of the King, the richest men in the kingdom.

Richard and John didn't even bother to pay the rent on their farm. Their mean and miserly landlord could have it back for all they cared. Instead, they bought a new farm next to a stream, where the land was well watered and fertile.

News of the brothers' adventure spread throughout the land. The King decided to make them knights. When one of the King's ministers objected that the King couldn't make knights of commoners, the King replied that the brothers had proved worthy of knighthood by slaying the phoenix and fulfilling their quest. "Besides," said the King, "our kingdom is completely out of knights. We can't be too picky."

Sir John and Sir Richard became very great knights. They selected and trained a whole new generation of knights to serve the King and his people. But they didn't limit their training to only men and women of noble birth. All the kingdom's people—even peasants, farmers, and other common folk—were eligible to become knights as long as they were good, honest, and brave.

When the brothers happily retired to their farm in old age, they took great pride in having lived a life full of good deeds and service. They knew their father would've been proud.

A Pirate Never Forgets

Author's Note: Be prepared to tell stories about events going on in your children's lives. For example, when the movie "Pirates of the Caribbean" came out in theatres, all my kids wanted to hear were stories about pirates. Here is the pirate story I came up with the night after we saw "Pirates" at our neighborhood theatre.

THIS IS THE STORY OF ONE MEAN PIRATE named One-Eyed Sam, and an even meaner pirate named Black Bill. One-Eyed Sam and Black Bill were sworn enemies. How did they get that way? It all started the day that One-Eyed Sam earned his nickname.

One stormy evening, in a tavern in the Jamaican town of Port Royal, One-Eyed Sam was playing Black Bill and some other pirates in a game of cards. The night was humid, and the smoke from the pirates' cigars and pipes hung heavily in the air. Along past midnight, only One-Eyed Sam and Black Bill were left at the card table. Maybe they drank too much rum that night, or perhaps they were just tired and cranky, because they got into a fight. Black Bill accused One-Eyed Sam of cheating at cards. One-Eyed Sam drew his sword. But Black Bill was a step ahead and pulled out his pistol, which he aimed directly at the space right between Sam's eyes.

For several seconds both men froze. The entire tavern went quiet. Who would make the first move? Just when many in the tavern thought the two pirates would back down, Black Bill snapped his pistol's trigger. The pistol erupted into flame and smoke.

A bullet fired at such close quarters would mean the end of most men, but Sam was quicker than most. Sam knew what an ornery ole 'cuss Bill was. Right from the start Sam had no doubt that Bill would try to shoot him. That was why Sam moved his head to the side a milli-second before Bill pulled the trigger.

Still, Sam didn't escape injury. The bullet, which by all accounts should've hit Sam right between the eyes, instead grazed Sam's left eye as he turned his head. Sam lost the

use of his left eye and had to wear a patch over it for the rest of his life. But at least Sam still had his life, and a lifetime, to plan his revenge on Black Bill.

Once Black Bill fired his pistol, bedlam broke out in the tavern. Everyone started fighting, breaking bottles, and firing off their pistols. In the confusion, Sam's crew managed to carry him out of the saloon to safety, before Black Bill could finish him off.

Sam and his crew left in their ship, *The Phantom*. They sailed to a safe port where they could plot their next move. Ole Sam, whom everyone now called One-Eyed Sam, had no sooner recovered from his injury than he began plotting a way to get back at Black Bill.

Sam talked to himself as he paced the deck of his ship. "I must lure him into a trap. But what shall I use as bait?"

Sam stroked his beard, deep in thought. "In order to select the right bait, you have to figure out your prey's weakness."

Several more minutes passed as One-Eyed Sam kept pacing. Then the answer came to him. "Of course," Sam said, "it's obvious. Black Bill's weakness is his greed for gold. That's why he got into a fight with me that night at the tavern. He knew I was winning at cards, and he didn't want to lose."

Now that One-Eyed Sam knew how to lure Black Bill into his trap, the rest of the plot came easily. Sam had his crew spread a rumor in all the ports of the Caribbean that a Spanish galleon, laden with gold, had run aground on a deserted island during a bad storm. The island was called Dead Man's Reef. According to the rumor, the island wasn't on any maps. No one knew its location.

Before long, every pirate, bounty hunter, and brigand in the entire Caribbean was looking for Dead Man's Reef. It was a fool's errand, because there was no such place. Not, that is, until One-Eyed Sam got around to creating one.

That's when Ole Sam put into motion the next stage of his plan. He sent one of his sailors, Scurvy Dan (who was unknown to Black Bill) to Port Royal. His instructions were to get into a card game with Black Bill. Scurvy Dan did just as he was told, even though he didn't understand Ole Sam's next order.

"Are you telling me you want me to lose in cards to Black Bill?" asked Dan.

"Exactly," said One-Eyed Sam. "And when you've lost all your money, bet this." Sam handed Scurvy Dan a rolled-up chart.

Scurvy Dan unrolled the chart and studied its contents. "It looks like an ordinary map to me."

"Not just any map," said Sam, "but a map showing the location of Dead Man's Reef."

"You mean such a place really exists?"

"Of course not," said One-Eyed Sam. "I just drew this map myself. The island I've marked as Dead Man's Reef is known to no one except me. It doesn't even have a name, it's so tiny. But it's going to help us catch Black Bill. Now all you have to do is lose this to Bill in a card game."

And that's exactly what Scurvy Dan did. He purposely lost all his money playing cards with Black Bill. When Dan had no money left, he begged Bill to play one more hand so that he could have a chance of winning it back.

"But you have nothing to wager," said Black Bill to Scurvy Dan. "Be gone with you!"

"I have no more money," said Dan, "but I do have this." He pulled Sam's chart out from inside his boot. "This," continued Dan, "is far more precious than money alone. It's the map showing the location of Dead Man's Reef."

"The place where the Spanish galleon ran aground with all her gold aboard?" asked Black Bill in astonishment.

"The one and the same," replied Scurvy Dan, knowing that he had set the hook just right. Black Bill let Scurvy Dan back into the game at once.

And just as quickly, Black Bill won the next hand (or rather, Scurvy Dan let Bill win it), and the chart was now Bill's. Bill wasted no time provisioning his ship and assembling his crew. In two days, he and his ship were under way, in search of the mysterious Dead Man's Reef.

One-Eyed Sam's spies kept an eye on Black Bill. Meanwhile, Sam made ready. First, he had some pirating to do on his own. Sam and his crew seized a Spanish merchant ship heading out of Santo Domingo for Spain. Once Sam had captured the ship, he ran it aground on the little island he had renamed Dead Man's Reef. There he scattered some of the ship's treasure on the sand around the beached ship. But he left a chest of gold inside.

Next, One-Eyed Sam sailed his own ship, *The Phantom,* into a hidden cove on Dead Man's Reef. He made sure *The Phantom* couldn't be spotted from sea, and waited for Black Bill to take the bait.

It didn't take long. With his greed driving him on, Black Bill and his ship arrived that same afternoon. Bill anchored his ship off shore, and took most of his crew in longboats to search the wrecked treasure ship. "The rumors were true," said Bill to his crew. "There really is a Dead Man's Reef, and a treasure ship run aground. I can't believe my own good luck!"

But his luck was about to turn. Once Bill and his party had landed on shore, One-Eyed Sam set the trap. He hoisted his sails and brought *The Phantom* out of the cove. With guns blazing, *The Phantom* quickly sank Black Bill's ship and his longboats. The survivors jumped overboard and swam to shore, joining Black Bill and the rest of his crew.

One-Eyed Sam had Black Bill just where he wanted him. Black Bill was stranded on a deserted island with no provisions or weapons. When Black Bill saw *The Phantom,* he knew he had been outsmarted. He readied his crew for the cannon barrage that would surely follow.

"Captain," said One-Eyed Sam's first mate, "shall I give the order to commence firing?"

"No," said Ole Sam. "Stow the cannons, and set a course for Port Royal."

"But Captain," said the first mate, "aren't we going to finish off Old Bill?"

"We don't need to," said One-Eyed Sam. "We've left him to a fate far worse than death. Black Bill's greed led him into our trap. His lust for gold is what got him into this fix. And strangely enough, he got what he came for. All the gold to make Bill rich three times over is in that shipwreck. He has all the gold his heart desires. But it does him no good because there's nowhere for him to go and nothing to spend his gold on. It's Black Bill's worst nightmare. Set sail now and leave that black-hearted Bill to his fate."

The sailors saw the cruel wisdom in One-Eyed Sam's plan and gave him a big cheer. They set sail, and the wind carried *The Phantom* quickly away from Dead Man's Reef. Before long, the island—with Black Bill marooned on it—was just a speck on the horizon.

64

Worth Every Penny

Author's Note: No stories are more charming than folk tales. They are simple and understandable, yet compelling in their logic. Folk tales can be funny or ironic, but are always full of valuable lessons and relevant to daily life. The folk hero often delivers his message in an unexpected but effective way. The most entertaining stories are those where the listener can't tell whether the folk hero is wise, foolish, or both.

The idea for the following story came from one of those string e-mails everyone receives from friends who admit they have too much time on their hands. You know these e-mails . . . the ones that offer endless top ten lists, jokes, pictures of cute animals, bad poetry, political commentaries, or inspirational life stories. Avoid the inclination to delete these e-mails without reading them; they often contain a gold mine of ideas for good stories.

I tried to convey the common sense wisdom of the Old West in this story about a traveling salesman who understood that weak-minded, gullible, and greedy people make the best customers.

THERE ONCE WAS A SMALL FARMING TOWN in the Dakota territory in the days of the Old West. The most respected man in town was the circuit judge, the Honorable J.T. Swift. All the townsfolk looked to Judge Swift for advice and counsel.

One day, a traveling salesman came to town. He went to the well in the center of town and began telling the townspeople that he had a miraculous thing to sell. Soon a large crowd gathered.

Holding up a cloth bag, the salesman reached inside and pulled out a handful of gold-colored seeds. "Not just any seeds, mind you," he said. "Magic seeds. They grow flowers that shoot out gold dust like pollen. That's right. You heard me. Real gold dust!"

The crowd was astonished. "That's impossible," said Dusty Hickok, a local rancher. "No such thing exists."

"Then look at this," said the traveling salesmen, who expected this response. He pulled from his coat pocket a pouch and poured its contents onto a plate. "Real gold dust!" He held the plate for all to see. On the plate was a mound of golden powder.

"Sure looks like gold dust," said Mildred Cassidy, a seamstress in town.

Jesse Custer, the owner of the local dry goods store, agreed. "Yeah, it does. But how do we know this gold dust came from flowers grown from your seeds?"

"Prove it to yourselves," said the salesman. "For fifty cents apiece, I'll sell you some seeds. If—in just one day—the seeds don't grow flowers filled with gold dust, I'll give you your money back."

"We don't even know your name," called out the Widow Grimsley.

"The name's Smith," said the salesman, "but my friends call me Sonny."

"Well, Sonny," continued Mrs. Grimsley, "how will we find you?" She adjusted her wire-rimmed glasses on her nose so she could better see the salesman.

"I'm camping in the grove of trees by the river. You can find me there."

The townsfolk didn't quite trust this traveling salesman. Still, it was tempting to buy seeds that would sprout flowers filled with gold dust. They turned to Judge Swift for advice.

"Judge, does paying this man fifty cents for the golden flower seeds seem like a good deal to you?" (Now remember, fifty cents in those days was a lot of money.)

The Judge thought for a moment before replying. "Yes, I think it's a very good deal."

With that, just about every person in town paid the traveling salesman fifty cents for seeds. They immediately rushed home, planted the seeds in their vegetable gardens, and watered the seeds with care. Then they sat down to wait.

One hour, two hours, three went by. Soon, a day passed, and no flowers had sprouted. To be sure, they waited a full two days before giving up on the seeds.

"Let's go to the grove by the river," said Dusty, "and get our money back."

"Count me in," said the Widow Grimsley. Soon all the townsfolk who paid the salesman marched down to the river to confront him.

When they arrived at the grove of trees, there was nothing—and no one—to be found. The salesman had run away. Not even a burning coal from his cooking fire was left behind.

"This is all the Judge's fault," said Jesse. "Yes," said Mildred, "it was the Judge who told us to do the deal."

The crowd marched back to town and gathered around the Judge's office. "What's this all about?" asked the Judge as he appeared at the front door of his office.

"It's all your fault," said Jesse. "The salesman cheated us of our money. The seeds he sold to us were worthless. When we went to the river to look for him, he was gone."

"Yes," cried Mildred, "the salesman was a liar, a cheat, and a fraud. He stole our money. Now we will *never* see him again."

"Never see him again; isn't that something!" muttered the Judge to no one in particular.

Dusty pointed his finger at the Judge. "And you're to blame. You're the one who told us it was a good deal."

"And so it was," said the Judge.

"What do you mean?" asked Dusty. "We paid good money for those seeds. And they were worthless. How do you call that a good deal?"

"I didn't say buying the seeds was a good deal," replied Judge Swift. "I said that paying the salesman was a good deal."

"How can that be?" asked Mildred. "We'll never see that no good, lying, cheating, stealing rascal again!"

"In that case," said the Judge, "the seeds you bought were worth every penny!"

By connor

68

The Gamekeeper, the Falcon, and the Rabbit

Author's Note: I always urge my children to respect others, especially those kids in class who aren't the most popular. Instead of admonishing my children with the Golden Rule, I came up with the following story with my sons to remind them that even the littlest, meekest, and seemingly most insignificant creatures have feelings and are deserving of respect.

I N A KINGDOM LONG AGO, there lived a gamekeeper named Clarence. Clarence served the King, looking after the King's hunting preserve and making sure everything was in order when the King went hunting on his lands.

Though he worked for the King, Clarence was still very poor. That is because the King was a miserly old man. He cared nothing for his subjects, let alone his servants. Clarence often had trouble finding enough food for his wife and their six children. Still, life was not always bad for Clarence and his family. They liked living in the country and made the forests and fields their home.

Though poor, Clarence had one prized possession, his hunting falcon, Magic. Years before, the King had given Magic to Clarence. Magic had accidentally broken a wing and the King didn't want him anymore. Clarence healed Magic's wing and before long, Magic was as good as new. So good, in fact, that Magic soon became the best hunting falcon in all the King's lands.

The King used falcons to hunt for sport. That meant he hunted with falcons for the sheer pleasure it gave him. For Clarence, hunting with falcons (or falconry) was a more serious affair. Clarence needed Magic to find food for his family. Because Magic was such a good hunter, he caught something every day for Clarence's family to eat. Grouse, pheasants, squirrels, and Clarence's favorite, rabbit. Magic was especially good at catching rabbits. And Clarence was especially good at making them into delicious stews. Were it not for Magic, Clarence's family would likely have starved long ago.

One day, as Clarence was walking through the fields around dusk with Magic perched on his forearm, he saw a rabbit in the next field. The rabbit popped his head up from his burrow, and Clarence immediately let Magic loose. After circling in the air, Magic dived to the ground at the exact place where Clarence had seen the rabbit. Magic appeared to be wrestling with something, so Clarence ran towards him in the hope that he had caught another plump rabbit.

But it wasn't a rabbit Magic wrestled with. It was something else. As Clarence got closer, he saw that Magic had in his talons a shiny object. Clarence bent over to pick it up and discovered to his amazement that Magic had found a small bar of silver. Clarence couldn't believe his good fortune. He could sell the bar of silver and make enough money to feed his family for a whole year! And his good fortune was all due to Magic.

A week later, Clarence was back in the same field hunting again with Magic. Just as before, Clarence saw a rabbit. Clarence released Magic into the air. After briefly circling, Magic dived to the ground at the same spot where Clarence had seen the rabbit. Again, Clarence saw Magic wrestling with something. When Clarence drew closer, he discovered that Magic had found another shiny object. This time, though, it was gold.

Clarence jumped into the air with happiness. "How can I be so fortunate twice in one week?" he shouted. "With this bar of gold, I'll be able to feed my family for two years. Magic," said Clarence, "I have you to thank."

But Clarence's luck didn't stop there. A week later, the same thing happened again. But instead of silver or gold, Magic found a bar of platinum. Platinum was worth even more than gold, enough to feed Clarence's family for five years. Clarence said to Magic, "You really are a magic bird. How else could you find all these precious gifts for my family?"

Then a voice from behind Clarence whispered, "It's not only the falcon who is magic."

Clarence whipped around. "Who said that?" he asked.

"I did," said the voice.

"Where are you?" asked Clarence. "Come out of your hiding place so that I may see you."

"But I am out of my hiding place," said the voice. "I'm right here in front of you."

Clarence looked down by his feet. There he saw a small, gray, furry rabbit! "What . . . I mean, who, are you?"

"I'm a magic rabbit. I've been digging up silver, gold, and platinum bars from my many burrows, and then leaving them for you and your falcon to find."

"Why would you do that?" Clarence couldn't believe he was talking to a rabbit.

"Because I know why you hunt my friends and me," said the rabbit. "You're poor and have nothing else to feed your family."

Clarence didn't know what to say. His shoulders drooped, and he looked down at the ground.

The rabbit continued, "I give you these treasures so that you may sell them to buy food for your family. That way, you'll never have to hunt rabbits again."

Clarence looked into the rabbit's eyes. Clarence realized that hunting for his family had come at a cost to another's family. He also realized how fortunate he was to receive the gifts of silver, gold, and platinum.

Clarence thanked the rabbit. From that day on, he never hunted rabbits or any other living creature again. Instead, he taught Magic how to hunt and fetch small balls he threw out into the fields. And whenever Clarence needed food for his family, he simply walked out into the fields at dusk. If he saw a rabbit poke his head out of a hole, or from around a bush, he knew that a treasure was nearby for Magic to find.

I Want My Magic TV

Author's Note: On nights when I really want to test our creativity, I challenge my sons to a game of speed storytelling. Speed story is our shorthand phrase for a contest we play in which we take turns making up stories as fast as we can. What makes this contest so much fun is that, like combination stories, each of us suggests a character or a subject that has to be included such as an animal, a person, or an object, until four are chosen. We then take turns speed-telling a different story using the same four characters.

One evening, my older son Will started with "elephant," my younger son Connor came next with "Godzilla," and I followed up with "cave man." Again, we each blurted out the very first word that popped into our minds. Will rounded out the four subjects of our story with—of all things—a "90 inch plasma HD TV." (Will wanted a flat screen TV for the family for Christmas.)

"Let's see," I said aloud, "a story with an elephant, Godzilla, a cave man, and a 90 inch plasma HD TV." Talk about four unlikely subjects! Allowing myself no further pause, I made up the following story in record time.

BOB WAS IN THE MARKET for a new TV. He was tired of his old antenna television that always went fuzzy at the first sign of a thunderstorm, or near the end of a tied football game. He wanted one of those big, fancy, flat screen TVs.

The problem was, Bob didn't have much money. Flat screen TVs were very expensive. Too expensive for Bob.

On Saturday mornings, Bob walked to his neighborhood appliance store to look at the new TVs on display. And every Saturday afternoon, Bob walked back home, empty-handed and feeling dejected.

One Saturday, as he returned home, Bob walked past a new storefront. A painted sign on the front window announced, "TVs for sale." Bob looked inside. There was nothing in the store except one television, sitting by itself on a stand. But what a TV! It had a 90 inch, high definition, plasma screen. With a TV like that, Bob could watch football games to his heart's content.

"Why don't you come inside for a better look?"

Who said that? Bob looked to his right. There, standing in the store's doorway, was an odd looking man. He was fifty-ish and wore a pencil thin mustache. He had jet black hair, slicked down and parted in the middle. He was dressed in a flashy pinstripe suit with a lavender silk handkerchief sticking from his pocket.

"Who are you?" asked Bob.

"My name is Phil. I'm the salesman here. Are you in the market for a new TV?"

"Maybe. It depends on how much it is," said Bob.

"Then I've got a deal for you. Come on inside." Phil gestured for Bob to enter.

Bob hesitated for a moment. "I guess it won't hurt to look," he said as he entered the store.

Phil used a remote to turn on the TV. It was the best picture Bob had ever seen. "So life like," he muttered.

"And it comes with a thirty-year warranty," said Phil. "Along with free delivery and hook-up."

"How much does it cost?" asked Bob. He tensed for the bad news.

"That's the best part," said Phil. "It only costs $500."

"That's a great deal," said Bob, feeling relieved. A frown then crossed his face. "Wait. It isn't stolen, is it?"

"Absolutely not. I'll give you a bill of sale. And a money back guarantee. No questions asked."

"You've got a deal." Bob was very happy.

As Bob was paying for the TV he asked, "By the way, who makes this TV?"

"It's a new manufacturer from overseas," said Phil. "The Magic TV Company."

"Hmmm," thought Bob as he left the store. "I've never heard of it."

Workmen delivered the TV and installed it in Bob's house that same day. Bob turned it on. The picture was even better than it was in the store.

Bob, like most guys, loved to channel surf. His first stop was the Explorers' Channel. He watched a show about cave men. The show had actors dressed like Neanderthals, portraying what life was like for some of our planet's earliest inhabitants. The cave men looked so real. They almost jumped out of the screen.

At that moment, one of the Neanderthals did just that. He jumped out of the TV into Bob's living room. He was covered in hair, wore animal skins, and carried a big club. The Neanderthal looked around the room, then glared at Bob. He grunted and raised his club.

Bob was terrified. He drew his body into a ball and sat shaking and cowering on the couch.

Luckily for Bob, an ambulance passed by with its siren blaring. The noise startled the Neanderthal. He covered his ears and ran out the door.

The Neanderthal left as quickly as he had come. So quickly that Bob wasn't even sure if what he had seen was real. He rubbed his eyes and looked around the room. Everything was quiet. Only the ticking of the hall clock over the drone of the TV could be heard. Maybe he had just fallen asleep and only dreamed about the cave man.

Time to change the channel, Bob thought. He turned to Animal World. There was a nature program on about Africa. Thousands of animals were grazing on the savannahs of East Africa. Giraffes, zebras, antelopes, and elephants. One close-up showed a cute baby elephant playing with his mother. "Ah!" said Bob, as he kicked his feet up on the couch. "This is much better."

But not for long. In the next instant, the baby elephant jumped from the screen onto the floor next to Bob. Bob's eyes grew as big as saucers. The elephant raised his trunk and tickled Bob around the neck. "Cut that out," said Bob. As he squirmed to get away, he glanced back at the TV. What he saw next drained the color from his face.

Lions!

"I've got to change the channel before those lions jump out." Bob searched frantically for the remote. Where was it? He checked between the cushions. No remote. He looked on the table next to the sofa. Nothing there. All the while, the elephant kept tickling Bob with his trunk. "You're so annoying," he shouted.

Bob looked under the couch. There it was! He grabbed the remote, pointed it at the TV, and clicked. Nothing happened. Whoops! He had it turned the wrong way. The TV picture had now zoomed in on a big male lion. He had to hurry. Bob pointed the remote again and randomly pushed a button. To his relief, the channel changed.

"That was close!" Bob collapsed onto the couch. The elephant, though, wouldn't leave him alone. It tickled Bob under the arms. Bob laughed and dropped the remote to the floor. Before he could snatch it back, the elephant stepped on it, crunching it into a zillion pieces.

"You dumb pachyderm," shouted Bob. "How am I going to change the channels now?"

Bob gasped. His eyes darted back to the TV. What would the next program be?

The voice of the announcer boomed. "You're watching the Science Fiction Channel. Stay tuned next for . . . 'The Adventures of Godzilla!'"

The Old Dead Horse

Author's Note: Take a story your own parents told you as a child—and make it new.

"The Old Dead Horse" is just such a story from my family. My mother claimed she adapted the story from a joke she heard at a holiday cocktail party. Over the years, she must have told it to me a hundred times, embellishing it a little with each telling. I never got tired of hearing it, and it still makes me laugh each time I tell it to my own children.

ONCE UPON A TIME, THERE WAS A MAN NAMED CHARLEY. Charley was a good fellow, but folks didn't consider him too smart. Everyone in his hometown knew this about Charley. In fact, some people called him downright simple. But Charley didn't care what people said. He always treated others kindly, and greeted everyone he met with a smile or a friendly word.

One day, as Charley was walking down Main Street, he saw two men loading a dead horse into the back of their truck. The horse had been very old and had apparently died right there.

Charley called out to the two men, whose names were Butch and Calvin. "Say fellas, watcha doin'?" Charley had a very nasal voice. When he spoke, he always sounded like his nose was stopped up.

"Well, Charley," said Butch. "What does it look like we're doing?"

"I don't know," said Charley. "That's why I asked."

"Charley," said Calvin (the more patient of the two), "this old horse died right here in the middle of the street. We're gonna take him in our truck to the town dump."

"You don't say," said Charley.

Butch rolled his eyes. Calvin smiled.

"I'll tell you what," said Charley. "Would you both like to make some money?"

"Sure," said Butch. "How much?"

"Fifty dollars for the two of you," said Charley.

"Wait," said Calvin, "what do you want us to do?"

"That's the good part," replied Charley. "I want you to take that old dead horse to my house."

"What would you want with an old dead horse?" asked Calvin.

"It's my business." Charley winked his eye. "Besides, fifty dollars is fifty dollars. What do you say, fellas?"

"Yeah," said Butch, "fifty dollars is fifty dollars."

"Well, okay," said Calvin, a little reluctantly. "If that's what you want."

Charley jumped into the cab of their truck, and together they drove to Charley's house, just outside of town.

"We're here, Charley," said Calvin. "What do you want us to do with this old dead horse?"

"Thanks for askin', fellas. Would you mind takin' it up to my second floor bathroom and dumpin' it in my bathtub?"

"Huh?" said Butch.

"Say again?" said Calvin. Calvin took off his cap and scratched his head.

"That's right, fellas," Charley said with a grin. "I want you to put that old dead horse in my bathtub."

"Wait just a minute here," said Calvin. "We are NOT going to put an old dead horse into your bathtub. Charley, have you lost your wits?"

"Nope," said Charley. "I know just what I'm doin'. If you'll do this for me, there's an extra fifty bucks in it for you." Charley took a hundred dollars from this pocket. He held it up in front of their noses.

Both men stared. One hundred dollars was a lot of money. And if some old kook wanted to spend his money this way, who were they to question his reasons. Or his sanity, for that matter.

The two men picked up the old dead horse. They carried it through Charley's front door, up the stairs, and into Charley's bathroom. There, they managed to lay the horse into Charley's bathtub, legs draping over the sides.

When they came outside, Charley was waiting. He counted out fifty dollars for each man. "Thirty, forty, fifty," said Charley. "It looks like we're all even now, fellas. Thank ya kindly."

"Thanks Charley," said Butch. "Fifty dollars a piece is a lot of money."

"Yeah, thank you Charley," said Calvin. "The money is very good, but . . ."

"But what?" asked Charley.

"Charley, I just can't leave here until I find out why you wanted us to put that old dead horse in your bathtub."

Charley chuckled. "I'd be glad to tell you."

"This I gotta hear," said Butch. The two men relaxed against the hood of their truck as Charley explained.

"Fellas? See that house right yonder next to mine?"

The men nodded.

"Mr. Smith lives there. He has been my neighbor for fifteen years. He's a real nice man. But if he has one fault, it's that he's so stingy. He won't buy a thing with his money. Cheap is what he is."

"How cheap is he?" asked Butch.

"He's so cheap," said Charley, "that he won't even put a real flush toilet in his home. Look out there in his backyard. That's an outhouse. In this day and age, Mr. Smith still uses an outdoor Johnny!"

"Go on," said Butch.

"It's the truth," said Charley. "Now, it's okay to use the outhouse in summer. But now it's winter and Mr. Smith doesn't like to use his Johnny when it's cold outside. Do you know what he does then?"

Both men shook their heads.

"He comes to my house about eight o'clock every night. He'll say, 'Charley? Can I use your bathroom?' And I'll say, 'Sure, Mr. Smith. Go right on up and help yourself.'"

Charley leaned closer to the men. "It wouldn't be so bad," he said, "if Mr. Smith just went upstairs and used my bathroom. But do you know what he does there that's so annoying?"

"What, Charley?" asked Calvin.

"He sits on that comfy toilet seat in my nice warm bathroom and thinks of real hard questions to ask me, just for the fun of seeing how dumb I am."

The men just stared at Charley, mouths open, not saying a word.

"It's the truth," said Charley. "Just the other night, he came down my stairs after using my nice warm bathroom. He asked me, 'Charley, who was the first President of the United States?' And I said, 'Oh, Mr. Smith. It makes my head hurt when you ask me such hard questions. You know I'm not smart. I don't know, Mr. Smith. Who was the first President of the United States?' He then said to me, 'Charley, you old dumb fool; it was George Washington.' Then he walked out of my house laughing."

"You don't say," said Butch.

"I do," said Charley. "Then a couple of nights later, Mr. Smith came down my steps after using my nice warm bathroom and said, 'Charley, what's the capital of France?' And I said, 'Oh Mr. Smith, you know I can't answer these hard questions, they make my head hurt. I don't know. What is the capital of France?' He said, 'Charley, you old dumb fool; it's Paris.' Again, he walked out of the house laughing, having made a nice joke on me."

"But, Charley" asked Calvin, "what does the old dead horse have to do with this?"

Charley pointed his finger up at the late afternoon skies. "See those dark clouds up there?" The men looked up.

"Feel that cold wind startin' to blow?" Both nodded.

"Well," said Charley, "it's gonna snow tonight. The wind's gonna blow, and the temperature will drop."

"If you say so, Charley," replied Butch.

"I guarantee it," said Charley. "I'll also betcha that around eight o'clock tonight Mr. Smith's gonna come over to my house. He'll ask, 'Charley, can I use your bathroom?' And I'll say, 'Of course, Mr. Smith. Just help yourself.'"

"So?" asked Butch.

"So," continued Charley, "while Mr. Smith is upstairs using my nice warm bathroom, I'm gonna wait right down here by the foot of my stairs. Do you know why?"

Butch and Calvin shrugged their shoulders.

"Cuz after a few seconds, Mr. Smith's gonna come stomping down those stairs just fit to be tied. And he's gonna ask me, 'CHARLEY! WHAT IN THE WORLD IS THAT IN YOUR BATHTUB?'"

The two men said not a word. They just looked at Charley with their mouths open.

"And I'm gonna say, 'Mr. Smith, you OLD DUMB FOOL, that's an OLD DEAD HORSE!'"

CULTURAL AND
HISTORICAL STORIES

The City of Frozen Canals

Author's Note: Tales from other lands, or from the past, never cease to instill in children—and adults—a feeling of awe and mystery. Stories from history or about other cultures open children's eyes, hearts, and minds to worlds beyond their own. Such stories have the power to transport, and to make the listener feel connected to the past or to the larger world.

On the day our family went ice skating for the first time, I was inspired to tell this story about a land where ice skating is more than just a sport.

THE COUNTRY OF HOLLAND is famous for its windmills, tulips, wooden shoes, and dikes. But its capital, Amsterdam, is famous for something else. The entire city is honeycombed with canals. During the warmer months, the canals are filled with boats taking the city's inhabitants to church, school, the market, and to its museums and theatres. But in the winter months, when it's very, very cold, the canals freeze. Everyone in Amsterdam knows what this means. Ice skating on the canals!

It's especially fun to ice skate on the canals at night. Streetlamps and torches light the way. People can skate for hours and never pass the same place twice. Vendors sell *poffertjes* (small, traditional pancakes) and hot chocolate from stands along the canal. When the canals freeze, Amsterdam becomes an impromptu winter festival, celebrated by almost all the city's residents.

Ice skating at night along the canals is especially fun for teenagers. The girls gather with their girlfriends, the boys band together with other guys, and the two groups warily eye one another. Occasionally, they mix as they skate. Jokes are exchanged, along with playful digs, and of course, a little flirting.

Anna was a young girl of thirteen who loved to ice skate. She liked a slightly older boy in her school named Hans. As Anna, Hans, and their friends skated the canals, Anna tried to talk with Hans. Hans was polite but didn't seem all that interested in talking to Anna. Anna was disappointed but tried not to let it dampen her fun.

At the central market district, the kids discovered that the shopkeepers had organized a speed skating race on one of the largest canals running through the district. In case you didn't know, speed skating is Holland's favorite sport. The first race was just for teenagers, but only for the very best skaters. Hans immediately signed up for the race. He was the captain of his school's hockey team, and also one of the best speed skaters around.

When Anna saw that Hans was racing, she decided to enter the race too, hoping this might impress him. All of Anna's friends were surprised to see her enter. They told her she was very brave to race such good skaters.

Hans wasn't impressed at all. "What are you doing here?" he asked Anna as she joined him at the starting line. "You're a girl. This race is only for the best skaters."

"So what if I'm a girl. All that matters is that I know I can beat you," said Anna.

"Oh no, you can't," said Hans. "Now get off the starting line and wait for the next race."

Anna's and Hans's friends started arguing about whether Anna should compete in the race. Maarten, the enterprising shopkeeper who was organizing the race, heard the hubbub and came over to investigate.

"What's this all about?" he asked good naturedly. "Why such harsh words on such a beautiful night?"

Hans told Maarten what the problem was. "A girl cannot enter this race. It's only for the best skaters."

"I am one of the best skaters," said Anna. "Just give me a chance and you'll see."

Maarten sized up the situation. Maarten was a bit of a sly fox, and soon came up with a clever solution.

"I detect that a wager is in order here," he said.

"What kind of wager?" asked Hans.

"Well, let's see." Maarten had a twinkle in his eye. "If you let Anna skate in this race and you beat her, then all the girls from your school have to buy the boys mugs of hot chocolate."

"And what if I win?" asked Anna. "What will the boys have to do?"

Maarten looked up at the full moon, then down at the teenagers gathered around. Everyone became quiet. "The boys have to give each of the girls a kiss under this beautiful moon."

"No way," shouted the boys. Hans's younger brother, Willem, said, "We're not taking that bet."

Hans's voice cut through the arguing. "We accept," he called in a clear voice. "Don't worry, guys," he added. "There's no way Anna will beat me."

The girls cheered. Hans reached out and shook Anna's hand. "You're on," said Anna.

The racers gathered at the starting line. There were twenty in all. A big crowd had gathered at the starting line and along the sides of the canal. This race would be a sprint, about one hundred meters. The crowd shouted encouragement to the racers before the start. Hans's friends were especially loud, shouting to Hans that he had better not lose this race.

Maarten was the starter. He stood at the end of the starting line and held a white handkerchief high into the air. All the racers had their eyes locked on Maarten as he began his starting cadence. "Ready, set . . ." he shouted clearly and slowly. When he at last said, "GO," and dropped his handkerchief, the skaters burst from the starting line. The race was on.

Hans took the early lead. He had a great start and felt very confident about his chances for winning. Anna had a slower start but quickly gathered momentum for the last fifty meters.

What Hans didn't know was that Anna had four older brothers, all of whom were champion speed skaters. They'd taught Anna how to skate and raced with her almost daily during the winter months. Most importantly, they showed Anna how to swing both her arms to build speed for the finish.

With twenty-five meters to go, Anna caught up with Hans. Now they both led the race. Hans looked very surprised to see that Anna had caught up with him. He gritted his teeth and quickened his pace.

But all the momentum was now with Anna. She'd carefully built her speed and caught up to Hans just when he thought he could coast to victory. At the finish line, Anna beat Hans by a stride.

The crowd cheered and clapped. Even Hans broke into a smile. He admired Anna's strong finish. Only Hans's guy friends seemed subdued. Maarten made them line up in a straight line opposite the girls in Anna's class.

"Now make good on your bets, gentlemen," said Maarten, grinning from ear to ear.

The boys hesitated, looking at their shoes. With a little more prodding from Maarten, each leaned forward and gave the girl opposite a kiss on the cheek. The girls giggled and cheered. They were pleased not so much with being kissed, but by the fact that the boys had lost the bet.

Then it was Hans's turn. Hans put his hands on Anna's shoulders, leaned forward, and gave her a kiss . . . on the lips! "Oooooh," went the crowd. Anna couldn't help but blush.

"Hot chocolate on me," said Maarten, feeling pleased with himself that he had orchestrated such a teenage love-fest. Everyone rushed over to his shop.

"Come on, Anna," said Hans, holding out his arm. "Let's go get some hot chocolate. I want to learn your secret formula for finishing a race."

"Hot chocolate, yes; racing secrets . . . maybe," said Anna. She took Hans's arm, and together they skated over to Maarten's shop to celebrate.

A Strange Visitor

Author's Note: Myths always make for colorful stories. The first myths were probably attempts by people to understand a world they couldn't explain. Over time, they became the sacred stories of a particular people's culture and history. As the following myth about Medieval Japan suggests, some miracles are bigger than we are and go beyond our understanding.

ABOUT A THOUSAND YEARS AGO, there was a small farming village in rural Japan. The people in the village were rice farmers. The farmers' lives were hard. They worked their rice fields (called paddies) all day long, knee deep in water, planting and harvesting their crops. Still, the villagers were happy. Though they were poor, they did have enough food to eat and fresh water to drink. Most importantly, they had each other.

Until misfortune struck. The rains stopped, and the land grew parched. The rice paddies and the nearby river dried up. With the water gone, the crops burned to a crisp. Soon the villagers had nothing to eat.

The villagers prayed to their local gods, spirits, and deities. They gave offerings of what little food they had to the deities of the sky, the rice paddies, and even the underworld. But most of all, they prayed to the water deities, particularly the river and rain gods.

Nothing happened.

Then one day, a stranger appeared in their village. He was very scraggly looking. He wore a long, unkempt beard, dirty rags for clothes, and his nose kept running. His behavior was strange. When the villagers asked the man for his name, his reply was always the same: "No-name." So that's what the villagers called him.

No-name told the villagers he was a very wise man who would be willing to exchange some of his wisdom and knowledge for a few yen. Yen is Japanese money.

"Money?" exclaimed the village mayor, a skinny man with a long mustache that drooped down to his collar. "We are poor peasants. We have no money. If we did, we

would gladly share it with you. But alas, our pockets are empty."

"Then how about a banquet in my honor?" asked No-name. "I'm starving and could eat a dinner cooked for twenty men!"

The village priest spoke up. He was an old man, with only a few wisps of white hair on his head. "We're poor, and in the midst of a famine. We have a little rice, which we're happy to share with you, but it will only be a handful. Still, you're welcome to it."

"But I'm also thirsty," cried No-name. "May I wash down your meager handful of rice with a jug of fresh water?"

Besides famine, we also have drought," said the mayor's wife, who was even thinner than her husband. "We have very little water. Our last well produces a few jars of water a day. Each of us must make due on half a cup of water. Still, we would be happy to share with you what little we have."

"May I at least have a place to rest my head? I dare not ask for a palace. I suspect none of you live in a home more luxurious than a hut. Am I right?"

"Yes, you're right," said the priest. "But however modest our homes, they're open to you."

For the next several days, No-name lived with the villagers, sharing what little food and water they had. At night, he slept on the floor in their huts, using a bit of straw for a pillow.

When No-name decided it was time to go, he packed up his few belongings. The villagers came in from the fields when they heard No-name was leaving.

"Wait!" said the mayor. "You promised to share your wisdom with us. And to help us with our problem."

"So I did," said No-name matter-of-factly. "Now, what's your problem again?"

The villagers were exasperated. They had shared their food and water with this stranger, and now he didn't seem to care. "Haven't you noticed?" said the mayor's wife. "We have so little food and water. The rains won't come, and our crops won't grow."

"Yes, of course," muttered No-name. "Here's what you need to do. Dig new wells for water. Repair the old ones. Make new water jugs from clay and new platters and dishes for all the food and fresh water you'll soon receive. If you do this, it will please the rain gods, and they'll send rain." Then he was gone.

The villagers were frustrated and confused. They debated what to do. "Why should we dig new wells when there's no water?" said one. "It's a waste of time." Another agreed. "Why should we make new jugs and platters when there is no water or food?" he complained. "What sense does that make?"

Several villagers nodded. "It's like building a cart when you have no horse," said the mayor. "What the stranger told us was a big lie. He came here, preyed upon our misfortune and took advantage of our hospitality. And if that wasn't bad enough, he gave thanks by playing a cruel joke on us."

Everyone shouted in agreement until one villager raised his lonely voice. "Wait," said the priest. "What do we have to lose by heeding the stranger's advice? We might as well dig wells and make new pottery jugs. If we believe with all our hearts that rain will come, this might please the rain gods. If what the stranger said is true, the gods will send rain."

All the villagers became silent. Finally, the mayor said, "The priest is right. Maybe doing as the stranger said will bring us good luck. Besides, we have nothing else to do."

And so, the villagers did just what No-name advised. They dug new wells, and cleaned out old ones. They built irrigation ditches and sumps and drains. They even fired up their pottery kiln and made new water jugs, plates, and bowls for all the fresh water and food they hoped would come in answer to their prayers.

Then a miracle happened. As soon as they finished working on the last irrigation trench and fired the last piece of pottery, the rains came. The rivers and streams roared back to life. The irrigation trenches and reservoirs quickly filled. The villagers celebrated by doing something they hadn't done in over a year. They planted a new crop of rice, along with lots of other vegetables. In no time, they once again had plenty to eat and drink. The villagers were proud that their hard work had brought an end to drought and famine.

Or had it?

From a hillside overlooking the village, No-name sat and watched the villagers. He smiled. He laughed. The villagers thought their work had brought back the rains. Their work did keep them busy, which kept up their morale and spirits. But it had nothing to do with the rains.

The villagers didn't know that No-name wasn't actually a vagabond. In fact, he wasn't even a real person.

"Silly villagers," said No-name, shaking his head. "Little did you know that I am the rain god! I came to your village in the appearance of a poor, sickly, and sometimes rude vagabond. Before I answered your prayers, I wanted to see if you were worthy of my help. Though you were poor, you shared what little food, water, and shelter you had. In return, I brought your village life giving rains. May you be blessed with bountiful harvests and prosperity to the end of your days."

The Repentant Samurai

Author's Note: Every now and then, kids come up with tough philosophical questions for their parents. One night, one of my sons asked me what karma meant. I have a hard time explaining that word to myself, let alone to a ten-year-old. Just as I was about to reach for the dictionary, I got an idea for a story that explained better than any wordy definition how a person's bad or good actions have real consequences.

THE SAMURAI WERE KNIGHTS who lived in Japan hundreds of years ago. They were warriors who took an oath of loyalty to the Emperor. They followed the Code of Bushido, under which they pledged to help the less fortunate such as the old, the weak, the poor, and the sick.

Once upon a time there was a young Samurai warrior named Katsu. Katsu was a very fierce warrior, skilled at *kendo* (sword fighting) and *kyudo* (archery). Although he had sworn an oath under the Code of Bushido to protect those who needed his help, he didn't follow the Code with all his heart. Deep inside, Katsu really felt that such people were weaklings and not worthy of his respect.

One day Katsu's lord commanded him to guard one of the roads leading out of the kingdom. The road was infested with bandits who had been robbing honest merchants of their money and goods. Katsu's job was to get rid of the bandits and make sure nothing blocked the flow of merchants bringing goods into the kingdom.

The bandits didn't stand a chance against Katsu. He simply walked down the road alone at dusk, knowing that the bandits couldn't resist robbing what appeared to be a lone, helpless traveler. As soon as the bandits surrounded Katsu, he pulled out his great Samurai sword and in no time defeated the bandits in hand-to-hand combat. Most bandits surrendered on the spot when they saw what a powerful fighter Katsu was.

After Katsu had gotten rid of the bandits, there was nothing much for him to do except

WM 2009

patrol the road. He didn't like this part of the job because he found it boring compared to fighting bandits. Sometimes, he took his unhappiness out on the people who used the road. He bumped into them and yelled insults, or made them bow to him as he passed. Other times, he helped himself to the fruits and vegetables they brought to market. Many of the merchants and villagers who used the road were afraid of Katsu. Though he was supposed to protect the common people, he acted more like a bully.

One day, he came upon an old man sitting in the middle of the road, blocking traffic. "Keep moving, old man," said Katsu. When the old man didn't respond, Katsu grew angry. "Get up and move, or I'll cut your head off."

"Do as you wish," replied the old man calmly. He neither looked at Katsu nor rose from the ground.

Katsu pulled his Samurai sword from his belt. "I'll give you one more chance to move," said Katsu. "Obey me, or die. The choice is yours."

The old man said nothing. He just stared ahead. "Then die," yelled Katsu. He swung his sword blade down on the old man's neck.

Whack! The sound of the impact was sickening to hear. As was the sight. The crowd that had gathered around Katsu gasped. Katsu ordered two villagers to drag the old man's body from the road and throw sand on the spilled blood. Though Katsu's voice sounded firm and in control, inwardly he was shaken by what he had done. He tried to justify his actions. "What more could I have done?" said Katsu. "After all, the old man deliberately disobeyed my order."

Katsu kept walking down the road. After a mile or two, he rounded a bend and gasped. There sat the same old man! Katsu couldn't believe his eyes.

"It can't be you," cried Katsu. "I just killed you."

"It would seem not," the old man said. Again, he didn't look at Katsu when he spoke.

This angered Katsu. "I don't know whether you're the same man or not. But I do know you're blocking the road. I've been commanded by my lord to keep traffic moving. Now get up and move!"

"I will not," said the old man, still looking straight ahead.

"Then prepare to die!" Katsu pulled out his sword and cleanly cut off the man's head.

This time, Katsu was more confused than shaken. He staggered down the road, dragging his sword behind him on the ground. He wondered how the old man had come back to life. Katsu came around another bend and there, to his astonishment, was the same old man sitting in the middle of the road.

Katsu rushed up to the old man. "How can this be?" he cried.

"What are you going to do now?" asked the old man, looking straight ahead. "Cut off my head a third time?"

Katsu was stunned. "I—I, I don't know what to do," he stuttered. "How can you come back to life after I've cut your head off?"

For the first time the old man looked directly into Katsu's eyes. "Because I'm not real."

"How can you not be real when I can plainly see you before me?" cried Katsu.

"Because I'm a figment of your imagination."

"What does that mean?"

"It means your mind is making me up. I'm like a dream to you. Or judging from the fear in your eyes, more like a nightmare."

"I don't understand." Katsu dropped to his knees and bowed his head.

"Your conscience is bothering you," said the old man. "You treat common people badly and don't respect them. So your mind is fighting back, causing you to see things that aren't real."

"What shall I do?" Katsu's voice trembled.

"Change yourself. Treat others with kindness and respect. Honor your oath as a Samurai to protect others, no matter how lowly or weak they are. Then, I'll go away. But remember, if you break your oath again, I'll come back."

"I understand," said Katsu, his head still bowed in respect. "I'll do as you command." When he raised his head to look at the old man, the old man had disappeared. Katsu turned around to see where the old man had gone, but no one was in sight. Katsu was alone.

From that day forward, Katsu did change his ways. He treated everyone with respect and kindness. He defended and protected the common people and those who needed help. True to his word, the old man never came back to haunt Katsu. But to the end of his days, Katsu never knew for sure whether the old man had been real, or just a figment of his imagination.

Why Do People Have Wars?

Author's Note: Use a story to explain a problem or event that has troubled your child.

One evening before bedtime, my older son William asked me why people have wars. The morality of taking human life is a difficult question for adults to answer and for children to understand. I tried to answer his question with a story showing that wars often result when hate and anger are passed from generation to generation. While cynics may argue that this has always been the way of the world, the following story—about two enemies forced to confront their own legacies—illustrates that hate and violence don't have to be the next generation's inheritance.

EVER SINCE PEOPLE HAVE BEEN ON THIS EARTH, they've fought with each other. Sometimes, so many people get involved in the fighting, the fights turn into wars. In war, people of one land fight the people of another.

It seems like it has always been this way. From the time people first gathered together to form towns, then cities, and later countries, they've fought wars against other peoples. It's still the same today. Somewhere in the world, at any given time, there's probably some type of war being fought.

A thousand years ago it was the same. At that time, the ruler of the River Kingdom, King Yorick, got into an argument with the ruler of the Mountain Kingdom, King Gavin. No one can remember what the argument was about, but before long a war broke out. Everyone prepared for war. Each king spent all the money in his treasury making weapons—swords, bows and arrows, armor, shields, axes—and trained his people to fight.

The people themselves gave up a lot. Instead of plowing their fields to grow food, or raising sheep for wool to make clothes, they spent their time training for battle and making weapons. But the people of each kingdom felt it was worth it. After all, hadn't the people from the other kingdom insulted them? A war would settle their disputes once and for all.

And so, the people formed armies, and the kings led those armies into combat. The two armies met on a great plain, and an enormous battle followed. For three days, the armies fought back and forth. Many people were killed. Many more suffered terrible wounds.

At the end of three days, both kings realized that sending more soldiers to fight was hopeless. But instead of calling off the war, they came up with another solution. The two kings would meet on the field of battle. With their armies gathered around them as witnesses, they would fight to the death. The victor could claim as his prize all the lands, wealth, and subjects of the losing king.

King Yorick and King Gavin started by fighting with swords. Both were excellent swordsmen, and neither could best the other. Every time one king thrust with his sword, or swung a monster blow, the other king blocked the attack with his shield.

They were such good swordsmen, both decided that the outcome couldn't be decided by a sword fight. So they switched to another weapon—the axe. Not just an ordinary axe, but a special kind. A two-headed battle axe. Again, because Yorick and Gavin were such excellent fighters, neither could defeat the other.

They next tried maces—sticks with a nasty metal object at the top used to club an opponent. Once again, neither could beat the other.

And on and on they fought. They tried spears, pikes, cross-bows, daggers, hammers, clubs, brass knuckles, even slingshots. The result was always the same. Stalemate.

King Yorick and King Gavin were so exhausted by all this fighting that they called for a rest. As they collapsed onto the ground, they heard a big commotion. The two kings gestured to their knights to step aside. As the knights cleared a path, Yorick and Gavin saw something that both amazed and frightened them.

There, off to the side, two young boys fought each other with sticks. Each was about four years old, and they came from opposing kingdoms. They used the sticks as pretend swords and tried to stab, eye-poke, slash, and smack each other. Just as their two kings had been doing.

"They're so young, only four or five years old," King Yorick said.

"Yes," said King Gavin. "I would ask how they learned to fight so furiously and with such hate, but I think I know the answer."

The two kings rose wearily from the ground. Together they walked over to the two children. Each placed a hand on the shoulder of a boy, and separated them from fighting. Then they took the sticks from the boys and broke the sticks in two over their knees.

In the snap of those sticks, the war between the two kingdoms ended. King Yorick and King Gavin signed a peace treaty and agreed not to fight any more. Instead, they set up ways to settle their differences peacefully. Signing the treaty wasn't hard. By then, they knew it was time to make peace. For it was their own small sons who'd been fighting one another with sticks that day.

A Silent Night

Author's Note: I always look for opportunities to share my love of history with my children. Historical events can form the foundation for a good story. As I often tell my children, history contains the best stories ever told, because no one could make up such spellbinding stories if they tried.

The following story is only one of two in this book that I didn't make up. It's based on a true story, one of the most poignant, yet uplifting events in history. Like the story before, "Why Do People Have Wars?", it deals with the subject of war and the taking of human life. It takes the form of a meditation, inviting the listener to contemplate how the human spirit endures even in the midst of suffering, fear, and hardship.

ONCE UPON A TIME, NOT SO LONG AGO, there was a very terrible war. This war was terrible because it lasted over four years, involved armies from many different countries, and ended only after many, many people were hurt or killed.

No one was quite sure how or why this war started. Had the people of one country insulted those of another? Had anger over past feuds simmered so long under the surface that it only took a spark to ignite this anger into war? No one knew for sure. In fact, people still argue today over why this terrible war began and whether it had to happen.

The soldiers of this war had to fight in horrible conditions. Each side developed new and terrible weapons. The soldiers sought safety and protection from these weapons by digging long ditches in the ground, called trenches. They cowered in the trenches to keep from being hit by bullets, shells, and bombs. Each army's trenches faced the other's. Because millions of soldiers were fighting, the trenches extended for hundreds of miles across the landscape. If you saw the trenches dug into the ground from an airplane, they looked like two, jagged scars running next to each other for as far as the eye could see.

To make matters worse, it rained most of the time. The rain turned the ground, already

dug up by bombs and fighting, into a muddy slime the soldiers had to sleep, eat, and fight in. Sometimes the soldiers stood for days in water and mud up to their knees. Rats were everywhere, as were the fleas and lice that constantly tormented the soldiers. The fighting was so intense it was often too dangerous for the soldiers to bury their dead comrades. The battlefield became a giant cemetery, as if all of mankind was doomed to die there.

Then, one night, something very rare and miraculous happened. The night was Christmas Eve. It was the first Christmas Eve of this long and terrible war. There was, thankfully, little fighting that night, and the whole battlefield was mostly quiet. The stars shone, and it was very cold. There was a dusting of snow on much of the battlefield. The soldiers huddled together in their trenches for warmth.

Suddenly, in the clear stillness of the night, some of the soldiers on one side of the battlefield began singing a Christmas carol. The soldiers on the other side held their collective breath and listened. They were amazed to hear singing when, just a little while before, they'd heard only the whizz and crash of bullets and shells. When the soldiers on one side of the battlefield finished singing, the soldiers in the opposing line of trenches began singing their own Christmas carols. "God Rest Ye Merry Gentlemen," "Oh Come All Ye Faithful," "Joy to the World," "Good King Wenceslas," and of course, "Silent Night." Back and forth went the singing. The soldiers took turns singing Christmas carols to those who, just a few hours before, had been their enemies. Many of the soldiers went to sleep that night in the glow of candles lit on small Christmas trees sent to them as gifts from back home. Others stared at the starlit sky in the light of lanterns they had strung across the tops of their trenches.

Christmas morning broke clear and cold. Would the soldiers resume their fighting after last night's singing? All the soldiers waited quietly in their trenches. When it seemed that no one could stand the waiting any longer, one soldier climbed out of his trench. He waved a white flag. The white flag is the age-old symbol of truce. The soldier did not wish to fight, but to talk.

Soon, other soldiers came out of their trenches. Many were just curious and didn't know at first what to say to the soldiers from the other side. Conversations often started when one soldier offered another some tobacco, or perhaps a treat from a Christmas package sent from home. Before long, many soldiers gathered between the trenches, sharing food with one another and exchanging souvenirs.

The tension between the soldiers had broken. A grizzled old sergeant began singing Christmas carols again. Others formed up teams and played a football match right there between the lines. Soldiers took time to bury their comrades who had died on the battlefield. Groups from both sides held a church service to remember those who had fallen.

At the end of the day, the soldiers went back to their trenches. The war, sadly, resumed once Christmas was over. But many of the war's survivors who were on the battlefield that very first Christmas Eve and Christmas Day of the war remembered it as one of the most special Christmases of their lives, as if they had been living in a dream. Looking back, it now seems almost impossible that the soldiers decided—at least for a few hours—to call off the war. But that's exactly what they did. In future wars, what if all the soldiers ordered to go to war decided on their own not to fight anymore? And what if we all treated every day as if it were Christmas? Then, perhaps, we would never fight another war.

GROWING UP STORIES

The Cleaning Lady

Author's Note: Never pass up an opportunity in your story to teach a lesson or a moral. Children are very curious about the world around them and are brimming with questions and concerns about growing up. Though they may feign disinterest, children carefully study the examples their parents set for them. Children welcome stories that tell a lesson or moral, as long as it's not too obvious what you're doing.

Storytelling is a great way to impart life's lessons to children without knocking them over the head with it. Parents can use stories to communicate their advice in subtle and indirect ways that don't threaten to awake that rebellious and contrarian streak lying within every maturing child or adolescent.

One of the most difficult lessons for children to learn (or for that matter, adults) is the importance of seeing the world through another person's eyes. Appreciating life beyond one's own narrow point of view teaches children how to get along with others, and prepares them to participate on teams, in class, and later, in the workplace. Though this is one of life's most important lessons, the following story demonstrates it's often one of the hardest to learn.

D ID YOU EVER stop to think how the bathroom in your school gets cleaned? Who cleans it? And how long it takes?

There once was a boy named Jeffrey who never gave a thought to this, except sometimes, to complain how long the cleaning lady in his school took to clean the bathrooms. When Jeffrey had to go to the bathroom badly, it seemed the cleaning lady was always cleaning the bathroom. The bathroom door was propped open, and Jeffrey noticed that same, annoying orange sign swinging from the doorknob of the bathroom door, which said, "Out of Order."

Did that make Jeffrey mad! He either had to walk to the other side of the school to use the bathroom, or worse, he had to wait until the cleaning lady was done. Oh, did she ever take a long time! He waited outside the bathroom door, twitching, rocking, and dancing from one leg to the other. Then, when she came out, he darted inside for blessed relief.

One day, when Jeffrey really, *really* had to use the bathroom, he rushed from his classroom, only to see the cleaning lady beat him to the bathroom by just a few seconds. Before he could squeeze out a "wait a minute," the cleaning lady propped open the bathroom door and hung that annoying orange sign, "Out of Order." As Jeffrey watched the sign swing back and forth from the doorknob, taunting him, the blood rose in his head, as did his temper.

AAAAGGHH, he shouted. "I've had enough of that sign and the cleaning lady!"

Jeffrey grabbed the orange sign and broke it in half over his knee. When the cleaning lady came out to see what had happened, Jeffrey threw the broken sign at her feet. He shouted certain words that no one should say to another person. He ran into the bathroom and dumped the trashcan on the floor. He danced merrily in the used paper towels. Then, he kicked them into the air and threw them in the sink. He used the bathroom, but didn't take care with his aim. What a mess!

And what a temper tantrum! It was bad enough that Jeffrey had lost it, but matters were about to get a lot worse. Guess who happened to be in the hall? The school principal, Mr. Long.

As soon as he saw Mr. Long, Jeffrey apologized and cleaned up the bathroom as best he could. But that didn't prevent a trip to the principal's office.

"Jeffrey," said Mr. Long, "the worst part isn't the mess you made, or your bathroom language. It's that you said such disrespectful things to Ms. Singleton. She has cleaned the bathrooms in our school for almost twenty years. She didn't deserve the treatment you gave her this afternoon."

Until then, Jeffrey didn't even know the cleaning lady's name. "I'm sorry. At least I cleaned up the mess I made in the bathroom." Jeffrey was thinking that straightening up the bathroom and making an apology would get him off the hook.

Mr. Long thought for a moment. "Jeffrey, while I appreciate your apology and the fact that you cleaned up the mess you made, I'm afraid that won't be enough. I'm going to give Ms. Singleton the week off. Guess who is going to clean the bathrooms while she's on leave?"

Jeffrey gulped. "Me?" he asked pitifully.

"Yes, you," said Mr. Long. "It will make you appreciate how much Ms. Singleton does for our school. You'll get to see things from her perspective for a change."

◆

Jeffrey's cleaning duties began the next day. He had to clean each bathroom (there were six of them) in the morning and after school. That made twelve bathrooms to clean each day!

The teasing from the other kids started right away. "Look everyone," said Melinda, "it's Jeffrey the Janitor. Don't forget to polish the mirrors in the girl's bathroom. I need a clean mirror to fix my hair after PE." All the girls in Melinda's clique laughed. Jeffrey growled under his breath. Melinda was the most stuck-up girl he knew.

But her teasing was light compared to Mickey's taunts. Mickey was Jeffrey's best friend. "Hey, Jeffrey," he called. "I think I forgot to flush. Can you handle that for me?" Mickey broke into sidesplitting laughter. How demeaning!

At first, the work was really, really hard. The other kids left things in such a mess. Paper towels littered the floor. Water and soap gunked the sinks. Lipstick writing on the mirrors. And Mickey wasn't the only kid who forgot to flush. Yuck!

The worst part of the job was cleaning the toilets. Kids weren't very careful when they went to the bathroom, and you can guess the results. Cleaning the bathrooms after lunch was really gross. "PeeeUuuu!" said Jeffrey, as he entered the bathroom. Jeffrey used one hand to clean the toilets and the other to hold his nose.

Gradually, though, the job got a little easier. Jeffrey developed a routine for cleaning the bathrooms. First, he'd pick up the trash so he could walk around more easily. Then, he'd go straight to the toilets and give them a good scrubbing with a brush and cleanser. Next, he'd tackle the sinks and mirrors. Of course, the more efficient he became, the less time it took him to clean each bathroom. What once took him two hours, now took him one.

At the end of the week, Jeffrey felt very pleased with himself. The bathrooms looked great. Even Mr. Long said so. When Jeffrey finished cleaning his last bathroom for the week, he stepped into a bathroom stall to put more toilet paper on a roll. Just then, a group of boys, led by Mickey, came into the bathroom. They couldn't see Jeffrey because he was still inside the bathroom stall. Jeffrey, though, could see all of them, and what they were doing.

The boys were pretty rowdy. They'd just finished a football game on the playground. They were hooping and hollering, being none too careful as to where they were peeing. On the floor, on the walls—you name it. They made a mess of the sinks and pulled most of the paper towels out of the dispensers. When they finally left, Jeffrey couldn't tell he had cleaned the bathroom a few minutes before.

At that moment, Jeffrey finally saw the world from Ms. Singleton's eyes. Ms. Singleton, his school's cleaning lady for almost twenty years, had to watch day after day as the students made a mess of her cleaning work. To make matters worse, a few even complained when they had to wait to use the bathroom while she was cleaning.

Quietly, Jeffrey set to work cleaning the bathroom again. He mopped the floors, scrubbed the toilets, and sponged down the walls and sinks. He carefully cleaned the bathroom mirrors again with cleaning spray and paper towels. When he finished, the bathroom had never looked better.

Just at that moment, Principal Long walked into the bathroom and gave it an admiring look. "Jeffrey," said Mr. Long, "I first had doubts that you'd last the entire week. But you lasted and did a marvelous job cleaning these bathrooms."

"Thanks, Mr. Long," said Jeffrey. "You were right about one thing. I was finally able to see what Ms. Singleton sees every day."

"Jeffrey," said Mr. Long, "I'm really proud of you."

"I'm proud of me, too." Jeffrey grinned. "And I know a few other boys who should clean the bathrooms next!"

The Boy Who Couldn't Decide

Author's Note: Busy parents need a way to connect daily with their kids and to find out what's going on in their children's lives. This can be hard to do, as every parent is familiar with the usual mono-syllabic responses from their kids to such questions as, "How was your day?" (Fine); and "What happened in school today?" (Nothing).

Storytelling provides that daily connection between parent and child. For example, try asking your child to pick an event, activity, or problem from his day to use as the subject of a story. If you do, you'll learn a lot about your child's day and what's on his mind.

One evening, one of my sons complained about how frustrated he got during the day when he couldn't make up his mind about the simplest decisions. Together, both my sons and I came up with the following story about a boy who had the same problem. When it came time to offer a solution to the boy's indecision, I let my sons suggest different endings. Letting your children decide the ending to a story always gets them more involved in the storytelling, but in this case, it also gave my son the opportunity to work through a problem.

THERE ONCE WAS a boy named Jack. Or if you like, you could also call him John, Jonathan, or even Johnny. That's because Jack couldn't decide which name he liked being called. With most things, Jack had a hard time making decisions.

One day at school, he went up to the ice cream counter after lunch to buy some ice cream. The ice cream vendor said, "What will it be, young man? We have two specials today . . . strawberry crunch, or chocolate chip fruity banana. Would you like one of the specials?"

"Yes," said Jack.

"Which one?" The vendor waited.

"What do you mean, which one?" Jack said.

"I mean, which flavor do you choose?"

"I don't know. I mean, it's hard to decide." Jack fretted.

"Hurry up, Johnny," shouted the other kids in line. "We want ice cream too."

JM
2010

110

"My name is Jack," Jack said.

"I thought your name was Johnny." One of the kids laughed.

"No, that was my name last week," said Jack. "This week my name is Jack."

"Whatever," said the kid. "Just hurry up and pick an ice cream."

"Okay," said Jack, "I'll take the strawberry crunch."

"Strawberry crunch it is," said the vendor.

"Wait," said Jack. "Make that chocolate chip fruity banana instead."

"You sure?" asked the vendor.

"Uh . . ." Jack hesitated.

"Why don't you step out of line while you decide, so that the other kids don't have to wait," said the vendor. "When you decide, you can get back in line."

"Okay." Jack stepped out of line. "I guess that will work."

By the time Jack finally decided, all the other kids in his class had bought their ice cream.

"I've made my decision," said Jack. "I'd like the chocolate chip fruity banana."

"I'm sorry, kid," said the vendor, "but while you were taking so long, the other kids bought all the ice cream. It's all gone. Maybe tomorrow, okay?"

Jack was disappointed.

That same day after school, a few of Jack's classmates came up to him on the playground. "John, would you like to play baseball or basketball with us?"

"My name is Jack," said Jack. "And yes, I would like to play with you."

"We thought your name was John," said the biggest kid, whom everyone called Moose.

"No," Jack said, "that was my name two weeks ago. This week, I've decided to call myself Jack."

"Whatever," said Moose. "Which game would you like to play, baseball or basketball?"

"I don't know," said Jack.

"Come on," said Moose's sidekick, Clancy. "It's your choice."

"Well, let me think about it," said Jack. "On one hand, I do like being the batter and hitting the baseball. On the other hand, I really enjoy dribbling a basketball. Geez, it's hard to decide."

Jack was taking so long to make a decision that Moose, Clancy, and the other kids lost patience. They went off by themselves to play . . . soccer! Jack was left out again.

That night, Jack sat at the kitchen table while his mom prepared dinner. Jack didn't talk, but only stared at a spot on the tablecloth.

Jack's mom watched Jack for a long time while she peeled potatoes. Finally, she spoke. "How was school today, Jonathan?"

"Please don't call me that."

"Call you what?"

"Jonathan," said Jack. "Jonathan is my full name. Now I just want to be called Jack."

"I see," said his mom. "What seems to be the matter with you today, Jonathan? I mean, Jack?"

"Well, Mom," said Jack, "sometimes I seem to have trouble making a decision. Have you ever noticed?"

"Oh, occasionally." His mom stifled a chuckle. "Did you have trouble making some decisions today?"

"Yes," said Jack. And he told his mother about what happened when he couldn't choose an ice cream flavor or a sport at school. "Why can't I make decisions for myself?" asked Jack.

Jack's mom untied her apron and sat down in a kitchen chair beside him. "I think I know what the problem is and what you can do about it."

"What?" asked Jack.

Can you guess what Jack's mom's advice was? [At this point, let your child offer some solutions to Jack's problem.] One of my sons first suggested that Jack say, "Eeny, meeny, miny, moe," before deciding. My other son said that Jack should tell the person asking him a question to decide for him. Here is the ending we all eventually came up with together.

"Well, Jonathan," said his mom.

"That's Jack," said Jonathan.

"Well, Jack," continued his mom, "I believe you're having a difficult time making decisions because you over think the problem."

"What does that mean?"

"It means that instead of making a decision, you go back and forth between all your choices, analyzing what is good and bad about each."

"You're right," said Jack. "Sometime I say over and over again, 'On one hand, I like this,' and then I turn around and say, 'On the other hand, I like that.'"

"Do you want to know a good trick to learn how to make a decision?"

"Sure," Jack said.

"Go with the first choice that comes to you," said his mom. "In other words, the first choice you *feel.*"

"I see," said Jack. "Today, when I first said I wanted strawberry crunch ice cream, I think a little voice inside was telling me it was the flavor I really wanted."

"Exactly." Jack's mom beamed. "That's a good way to describe it, as a little voice inside telling you what to do."

"When the kids asked if I wanted to play baseball or basketball," continued Jack, "I really should have said soccer, because that's what I really wanted to play."

"Now you're on the right track," said Jack's mom. "And once you've made your decision, stick with it. Don't ever second guess yourself."

"Thanks, Mom," said Jack. "I think this is really going to work."

"I'm so proud of you, Jack."

"And one more thing," said Jack. "From now on, I want to be called by my full name. The name you gave me when I was born—Jonathan."

"Are you sure?"

"I'm sure."

114

The Lost Guitar

Author's Note: Here's another story about one of life's little lessons, based on real events from our family's day. It was prompted by one of my sons who kept forgetting to take his musical instrument and his gym bag to after school practices.

AS HE WALKED HOME FROM SCHOOL, Mason tried to think of an answer to his problem. If he didn't find an answer soon, he was going to have to tell his parents what he'd done. He'd lost his guitar.

"How did I get myself in this predicament?" he asked. A voice came up from his conscience. "Mason, you got yourself into this mess because you're so irresponsible."

"I am not," said Mason.

"You're not?" said his inner voice. "Then what about soccer practice last fall?"

Mason's mind wandered back to last October. One day, Mason's parents picked him up from school to take him to soccer practice.

"Mason," asked his mom, "do you have your soccer shoes and uniform?"

"No, Mom," admitted Mason.

"Where are your shoes and uniform?"

Mason lowered his eyes and mumbled, "I guess I must've left them at school." Because he left his shoes and uniform at school, Mason didn't get to play soccer that day.

Mason said to his inner voice, "But that was the only time I forgot something."

"Oh, yeah," said his inner voice. "What about last week? With your homework?"

Mason's mind drifted back to Friday morning. Mason's parents had dropped him off at school. His mom asked, "Mason, do you have your homework?"

"I'm not sure," said Mason.

"Would you please check your backpack?"

"It's not there," said Mason. "I must've left my homework at home."

Mason's mom sighed. "You have to be more responsible. It's your job to remember your homework."

Mason's inner voice nagged more than his mom. "You see," said his inner voice, "it's your lack of responsibility that's gotten you into this new mess."

Mason said, "If only I could retrace my steps and figure out when and where I lost it."

Two days earlier, Mason went to his guitar lesson after school. "Hello, Ernesto," said Mason to his guitar teacher. Mason liked guitar class.

"Hello, Mason," said his teacher. "Are you ready for today's lesson?"

"I sure am," said Mason. "Let's get started."

"Mason, aren't you forgetting something?" asked Ernesto.

Mason looked confused.

"Where is your guitar?"

"I don't know," said Mason. "Excuse me, Ernesto. I'll be right back."

Mason dashed to his home classroom. He looked in his cubby. No guitar. He searched the coat closet at the back of the room. Empty. He then went to the principal's office to look in the lost-and-found box. Again, no guitar. That meant no lesson for Mason that day.

After school, Mason went home and searched his bedroom. Next, his playroom. Mason even searched his little brother's room. The guitar was nowhere to be found.

The next day at school, Mason searched every nook and cranny of every room in the building. Twice! Still, no guitar.

Now, as he walked home from school, Mason worried about what to tell his parents. Should he even tell them about the lost guitar?

"You need to tell them the truth," said his inner voice.

"Maybe if I bought a new guitar, I wouldn't have to tell them," said Mason. His feeling of relief only lasted a moment. "Who am I kidding? I'll never be able to buy a guitar. Guitars cost a fortune!"

"You need to tell your parents the truth." Mason's inner voice wouldn't shut up.

"I could borrow a guitar from Frankie or Isaac. My parents will never know I'm using one of my friend's guitars."

"Mason!" His inner voice was annoyed.

"You're right," said Mason. "Both Frankie and Isaac are taking guitar lessons this year and need their guitars."

His inner voice spoke more softly this time. "Mason. You know what you need to do."

Mason knew he had acted carelessly. His parents weren't wealthy. They had scraped together just enough money to buy him a guitar. There was only one thing left to do. Mason had to tell the truth.

"Mom, Dad," said Mason quietly at the dinner table that night. "I'm afraid I've lost my guitar. I'm so sorry. I know how much you saved to buy that guitar for me."

His mother paused before speaking. "Well, Mason, I have some good news for you. Your guitar isn't lost. Yesterday, after we dropped you off at school, we found your homework in the car. We drove back to school to bring it to you. We saw your guitar sitting behind a tree. You had left it on the playground. We decided to teach you a lesson and took the guitar back home. It's up in our bedroom closet."

That night, Mason lay in bed thinking. At first, he was mad that his parents' trick caused him to worry for no reason. Then he realized they'd only wanted to teach him a lesson. "Maybe I do need to be more responsible. No more losing my guitar, my homework, or my practice bag. I promise."

Mason waited for his inner voice to chime in. But his inner voice was already fast asleep.

The Real Karate Kid

Author's Note: Storytelling provides an excellent opportunity to reinforce good personal habits and to explain why it's important to work hard toward a goal. Both my children have long enjoyed the study of martial arts. When one of my sons complained, though, that he didn't feel up to martial arts practice the next day, we created this story to remind him about the purpose and benefits of learning self-defense.

FREDDY AND HIS FRIENDS had a problem with Doug. Doug was the class bully. He was easily the biggest kid in class. He was loud, pushy, and liked to pick on smaller kids, like Freddy. Doug was just plain mean. So mean that everyone called him Dog behind his back.

One day Freddy was waiting in the school cafeteria line when he felt a shove from behind. He turned around to see Doug standing there with a grin on his face. "What's going on, Chump?" Doug said.

Margaret, the girl Freddy liked, passed by on her way to drop off her cafeteria tray. "Doug, why don't you pick on someone your own size?"

Doug put on a show for Margaret. "He is my size. He just needs to be stretched out a bit." Doug picked Freddy up under his armpits. He raised him above his head. "See, now he's taller than me."

"Put him down," Margaret said.

"Whatever you say," said Doug. He carried Freddy over to a coat rack and stuck him on a hook. Freddy hung by his collar from the hook, with his feet dangling off the ground. "Maybe this will make you taller, Chump."

The school bell rang and all the kids, including Doug, skedaddled to their next class. Margaret found Mr. Skinner, the PE teacher, and together they helped Freddy down from the hook. Freddy wasn't hurt. His shirt wasn't even ripped. But the emotional pain he felt was far worse than any punch in the nose or black eye. Doug had embarrassed him before the entire cafeteria! Worse, Margaret had seen the whole thing.

That night at home, Freddy was unusually quiet. His mom tried to get him to say what the matter was, but Freddy refused to talk. It hurt too much.

After dinner, a commercial on TV caught Freddy's eye. It was an advertisement for a local martial arts studio. The commercial showed kids who were Freddy's age practicing some type of fighting. The kids were all fighting bigger opponents. They blocked punches, threw kicks, and flipped attackers to the ground. The last kid in the commercial was even smaller than Freddy. After knocking over a big bully, the kid looked into the camera and winked.

"That's what I need. If I can learn what they're doing on TV, then I'll be able to take on Doug in front of the entire class." Freddy grabbed a pen and wrote down "Master Kim's Tae Kwon Do Studio."

Freddy told his parents about the commercial. He begged them to let him take martial arts. His parents were easily convinced. They knew that Freddy had seemed down lately. They hoped that martial arts would boost his confidence and self-esteem.

Freddy showed up early for his first tae kwon do lesson. He was motivated by the hope that he would soon learn how to give Doug a good thrashing. The trouble was, Freddy wasn't even sure what tae kwon do was. He thought all martial arts were the same. Tae kwon do was probably the same as kung fu, Freddy thought. Maybe he could be just like Bruce Lee, beating six bad guys like Doug at once.

"Hello," said a tall Korean man with a shaved head. "My name is Mr. Kim, and I run this studio. May I help you?"

"Yes. My name is Freddy. I want to learn TAY KOOYAN DOO."

"It's pronounced TIE KWAN DOE. It means 'the way of kicking, blocking, and punching'."

"Cool," replied Freddy.

"Why do you want to learn tae kwon do?" asked Mr. Kim.

"Because I want to beat up a bully who's been picking on me."

"I see."

"Can you show me how?"

Mr. Kim thought for a moment. "Of course I can. But before you learn how to defend yourself, you need to learn the basics of punching and kicking. Once you do that, you will earn your white belt. Then we can discuss how to take care of bullies."

"Great," said Freddy. "I'm ready to get to work."

Mr. Kim showed Freddy how to stand and hold his fists. He demonstrated how to yell

"Hiya" in order to intimidate an opponent. Over the course of many more lessons, Mr. Kim taught Freddy how to do different kicks. Freddy was a good student. In no time, he earned his white belt.

"Now will you show me how to beat up that bully who's bothering me?" Freddy asked his teacher.

"Of course I will," said Mr. Kim. "But first, you must earn your gold belt."

"What's a gold belt?" asked Freddy.

"It's the next level after white belt. You see, there are many different levels of expertise in tae kwon do, each represented by a different color of the belt that students wear with their uniforms. The belts go all the way from white belt, which is for beginners, to black belt, which is for experts."

"After I get my gold belt, will I be able to beat up the bully in my school?

Mr. Kim smiled. "We'll see."

Freddy worked hard. He practiced and memorized many different combinations of fighting moves. Sometimes, he put on protective head gear and padded gloves and shoes so that he could fight other students in class. No one got hurt, and it was a lot of fun for Freddy to try his tae kwon do moves on another fighter. Freddy was a good student. Each time he earned a new belt, he asked Mr. Kim if he could learn how to beat up a bully. Mr. Kim always put Freddy off, saying he needed to earn his next belt.

Finally, the time came for Freddy to test for his black belt. The test was very difficult. Freddy had to perform by memory many different fighting moves in front of a panel of his teachers, including Mr. Kim. It took him almost an hour to complete his routine, and he was out of breath when he finished.

No time for a break, though. He next had to fight the other students in his graduating class. His teachers judged the fights. Each fight was three minutes long. The judges gave each fighter one point when they landed a punch, and two points when they scored with a kick. Freddy's first opponent was a kid his own size named Nelson. Nelson knew his fighting combinations, but he was a timid fighter. Freddy had to be aggressive.

Freddy and Nelson bowed to one another. Mr. Kim nodded, and the fight began. Freddy took the action to Nelson right away. He landed a front punch to the side of Nelson's headgear and scored one point. Nelson was shaken because Freddy had scored so quickly. He was then so worried about Freddy's punches that he never saw the sidekick that Freddy next landed to his chest. Two more points for Freddy. Nelson landed one punch of his own just before the fight ended, but it wasn't enough for him to pull out the fight. Freddy was the winner.

Freddy fought three more fights. He won each one handily. Mr. Kim was impressed. He instructed one of his older students, a black belt named Josh, to fight Freddy last. For the first time that day, Freddy was nervous. Josh was two years older than Freddy and at least a head taller. Worse for Freddy, Josh was probably the toughest fighter in the entire school.

As Freddy and Josh bowed to one another, Freddy's mind was racing. "How am I going to beat this guy? He's so much bigger than me." Freddy started off quickly with his favorite one-two punch. But Josh blocked Freddy easily with his left hand, and counter-punched with a jab to the side of Freddy's head. One point for Josh.

Freddy re-adjusted his head gear. He was angry at himself for letting Josh score so easily. "I know what I'll do. I'll pretend Josh is Doug. Nobody makes me madder and more determined than Doug."

Freddy looked at Josh and tried to picture him with Doug's face. Mr. Kim barked at the fighters to resume the fight. Freddy launched a fury of kicks and punches right at Josh's face. This was not allowed. For safety reasons, fighters were only allowed to land punches on the side of the head, which was protected by headgear. Freddy got so mad imagining he was fighting Doug that he forgot what he was doing.

"Break!" shouted Mr. Kim. "Punches to the face aren't allowed, Freddy. You know that. I'm awarding a point to Josh. The score is now two to nothing. Resume!"

Freddy was embarrassed because Mr. Kim had corrected him. He also lost his concentration. Before Freddy could re-focus, Josh nailed him with a side kick to the chest. The kick knocked the wind out of Freddy. Freddy bent over, hands on knees, trying to catch his breath.

Mr. Kim wasn't sympathetic. "Shake it off Freddy. You can't give up in the middle of a fight. Now is the time for you to earn your black belt."

Everyone in the studio watched Freddy. Freddy was still doubled over. He wanted to cry.

"Freddy! Look at me." Freddy turned his head toward Mr. Kim. "Use the lessons I've taught you. If you ever want to get rid of that bully, you can't let your anger or fear rule you."

Mr. Kim's words had a calming effect on Freddy. He straightened himself up, and raised his fists. Josh rushed in to finish Freddy off, but Freddy was ready. Josh threw the first punch. Freddy dodged it and landed one of his own. Josh tried a round kick to the side of Freddy's head. Freddy ducked, and scored with a jump kick straight into Josh's chest. Three points for Freddy. The fight was now so competitive that Mr. Kim ordered Josh and Freddy to fight three more minutes. At the end of the fight, both were exhausted. Josh ended up winning the fight by one point. But Freddy had won the respect of Mr. Kim.

And his black belt. At the end of the test, Mr. Kim tied Freddy's black belt around his waist in recognition of what a good student he was. "You showed me something today, Freddy. You showed me you could overcome your fear and anger. You gained maturity and confidence today."

"Thank you for everything you've taught me, Mr. Kim."

"Do you still want me know to teach you how to beat up that bully?" asked Mr. Kim.

"No," replied Freddy. "I don't think that's necessary."

Freddy was right. Doug never bothered Freddy again. It wasn't because Freddy beat Doug up. But he knew he could defend himself if he had to. After learning tae kwon do and Master Kim's many lessons, Freddy had changed. He walked around with a new, quiet confidence. He was no longer afraid of Doug. Everyone noticed it, especially Doug. Doug stayed clear of Freddy. Martial arts had taught Freddy how to handle bullies—without even having to throw a punch.

124

A Goth Christmas

Author's Note: Here's a story for maturing kids who are just starting to show some interest in (yikes!) the opposite sex.

HILLARY WAS A "GOTH." To some, goth is a style of dress. To others, it's a lifestyle. Like her other goth friends, Hillary wore black clothing and white makeup every day. She had her ears, nose, belly button, and tongue pierced. When her mother wasn't around, Hillary liked to wear black or crimson lipstick. Her hair was dyed raven black with purple highlights. She even had two tattoos. One on her shoulder, and the other—a butterfly—on her ankle.

Hillary listed to hard rock music. Her parents thought her music was bleak and depressing, but Hillary found that it reflected her mixed feelings about growing up. Hillary was a rebel. She never accepted rules just because someone else told her that's the way things are done.

Although Hillary hung out with a goth crowd, she liked a boy who was definitely not a goth. His name was Matt. Matt was a preppy. Being preppy is completely different from being goth. Matt was clean-cut and liked to wear polo shirts with khaki pants. He was president of his class and captain of his school's lacrosse team. During summertime, Matt enjoyed hanging around his parents' country club, swimming, and playing golf and tennis.

Although they were different, Hillary and Matt did have some things in common. Both were smart and caring, and worked hard in school. Most importantly, they liked each other. A lot.

Still, it wasn't always easy for two such dissimilar people to get along. Matt didn't like to hang out with Hillary's friends. He found them dull, lazy, and whiny. Hillary's friends didn't like Matt much either.

"Dump that guy," said Katrina, one of Hillary's best friends. "He's so law and order.

125

Besides, he just doesn't, well . . ."

"Well, what?" asked Hillary.

"Fit in," said Katrina. Katrina's comment hurt Hillary's feelings.

Hillary's other friend, Ashley, chimed in. "You should dump him first before he dumps you. He'll probably find some blonde, blue-eyed preppy girl he likes better than you, and then you're history."

It wasn't much easier for Hillary with Matt's friends. When Matt took Hillary to his friends' parties, Hillary stood out like a sore thumb. Matt's friends, though polite, gave her a wide berth. Hillary often stayed in the corner by herself.

"You could make an effort to talk to people," said Matt after they left one party.

"It's not my fault your friends are such snobs," said Hillary.

"Why do you always have to be a rebel? Couldn't you try just once to fit in with my friends?" Matt sounded angry.

"I could say the same thing about you. Maybe you need to try to fit in with my friends."

One word led to another. Before long, Hillary and Matt got into a fight. "Maybe my friends are right," said Hillary. "We just aren't right for each other."

"For once tonight, I agree with you," said Matt. "Maybe it's time we broke up."

"Fine with me," said Hillary.

"Fine with me," said Matt.

The next evening, Hillary told her friends that she had broken up with Matt. Her friends couldn't have been happier.

"It's about time," said Katrina.

Ashley agreed. "Let's go celebrate. I know about a great party across town."

Everyone had a great time at the party. Except Hillary. At first, she tried to convince herself that she was glad to be rid of Matt. But the more she thought about him, the more she realized how much she missed him.

Hillary woke up late the next morning. It was the first Saturday of the Christmas season. The stores had decorated their windows with Christmas ornaments and lights. A light snow was falling. Hillary loved snow. She decided to take a walk to cheer herself up.

She strolled along Main Street, stopping every now and then to window-shop. When she came to a beauty salon, she paused and looked in the window. She saw her reflection in the mirror and absent mindedly fiddled with her hair. She glanced up and down the street, took a big breath, and walked into the salon.

"Hello," said the salon receptionist. "May I help you?"

"Yes. I would like a complete makeover."

The receptionist introduced Hillary to a stylist named Olga. Hillary told Olga how she wanted to look. "Are you sure about this?" asked Olga.

"I'm sure," said Hillary.

Olga got right to work. She washed Hillary's hair, then began to cut. Where Hillary once had spiky hair, Olga gave her a stylish, bouncy cut.

"And for color?" asked Olga.

"Blonde," said Hillary. "No; wait. I want something closer to my natural hair color. Light brown. But with highlights."

"You've got it," said Olga.

Olga brought out her dyes and hair colors. While she worked, the salon's manicurist removed the black nail polish from Hillary's finger and toenails. Instead of black, she painted Hillary's nails a soft pink.

By this time, Olga had finished coloring and setting Hillary's hair. She held up a mirror for Hillary to see. "What do you think?"

Hillary stared for a long time into the mirror. The new hair style and color made her look softer. "Is that really me?" She smiled.

On the way home, Hillary couldn't resist a stop at a clothing boutique to buy a new dress. No more black clothes. Even though it was winter, Hillary picked out a short, flowery dress. When she held it up in front of a mirror, she stuck her tongue out. "How do girls wear these things?"

As soon as Hillary got home, she picked up the phone. She paused a moment, then summoned her courage and dialed.

"Matt? It's Hillary."

"Hi Hillary. I was just thinking about you," said Matt.

"And I was thinking about you. Can you come over? I have a surprise for you."

Hillary put on her new dress, borrowed a pair of her mother's dress shoes, and combed her hair. She heard a knock at the door. Before opening it, she checked her appearance in the hallway mirror. "Here goes nothing," she said under her breath.

"Oh, my gosh," said Matt. "You . . . you've changed." Matt couldn't believe how different—and beautiful—she looked.

Hillary was speechless.

"Well," said Matt, "what do you think?"

Hillary held her fingers to her lips, trying to suppress a laugh. "You've changed too."

What an understatement! Matt had dyed his hair black, with purple highlights, and was wearing a spiky haircut. He was dressed in black too, in a T-shirt, leather jacket, jeans, and high boots. He even wore an earring, but he admitted he couldn't muster the courage for one for his lip.

"You did this all for me?" asked Hillary, as tears filled her eyes.

Hillary wrapped her arms around Matt's neck and gave him a big kiss.

"Merry Christmas, Goth."

"Merry Christmas, Preppy."

Epilogue

The stories in this book resulted directly from the spontaneous, creative interplay between my children and me. What else explains why someone would write a story about feuding vampire and fruit bats, or Godzilla jumping out of an HD-TV?

How did you do? Did you read these stories aloud to your children to help you sense the magic that comes from original storytelling at home? Did you try creating some of your own stories with your family?

If you did try your hand at making up your own stories, you might want to give some thought to preserving them for your kids, as I have. Here are a few tips.

Preserving your stories

Initially, I didn't think about preserving the bedtime tales I was making up for Will and Connor. As a result, I lost about two year's worth of great stories. Don't let this happen to you! You can never re-capture those story gems. And I've found that if you don't memorialize your stories in some way—right away—you won't remember them.

The easiest and most obvious way to preserve your stories is with an electronic device such as a digital recorder, although I have to admit this didn't work for me. I tried a tape recorder, and the second I turned it on my mind froze. I couldn't come up with a single story line because I was so anxious thinking about the tape recorder.

In the end, I simply wrote my stories down. Not the full narrative, as that task seemed too daunting and time consuming. Instead, I jotted down the main elements of each tale using bullet points. That way, I wouldn't forget the central plot and characters and could use my bullet points later to write out the full text. But no matter what your method, the important thing is to memorialize your story in some way.

Once you've written out your collection of stories, it's great fun reading them over again with your children. You may be surprised how many of the stories your children remember, and you'll see first-hand just how much these stories mean to them. Better yet, present your written stories as a gift for a birthday or holiday. Long after they've grown up, your children will have a physical reminder of the fun times they had making up stories with you.

Storytelling as a family diary

Once you preserve the stories you tell your children, you'll find the collection becomes a sort of family diary in and of itself. Almost all of the stories included in this book have special meaning for my wife and children because they're created from actual events that happened—usually that very day—in the life of our family. For example, the day my children went ice skating for the first time, they wanted a bedtime story afterwards, and "The City of Frozen Canals" was born. "The Royal Bulldog" came from our family bulldogs, Spencer and Huxley, and "The Lost Guitar" resulted from my attempts to get the kids to remember to bring their gym bags and musical instruments to practices after school.

Although I regularly tell stories to my children and am fairly diligent in writing them down afterwards, I used to regret not keeping a diary to record daily or special events. Regretful that is, until someone pointed out to me that my collection of stories chronicled our family life in much the same way a diary would. Perhaps more so, since a story often describes a family event or adventure in a way that is more colorful or memorable than a simple diary entry.

The stories you create and preserve for your children will serve as a precious time capsule of their childhoods. Not only will they be a source of entertainment, but many will invoke sentimental comments from your children such as, "I remember that day." Or perhaps, "Did we really do that?" Or even, "Was it really that long ago?"

The wonder of storytelling

Always remember: the wonder of storytelling at home is that you will leave your children with a gift they will always treasure—the memory of spending time with you making up wonderful and fantastic stories. Years later, your children will remember your bedtime storytelling and the special times you shared. They will tell their own children and grandchildren what a great storyteller you were. You will have created a storytelling tradition in your family, and your kids will know just what to do when their own children and grandchildren ask them to "tell a story with their mouths."

◆

Afterword

A typical Friday night at home. It's long past the boys' bedtime, pushing 10:30 p.m. Dad is trying to get Will and Connor to go to sleep, unsuccessfully.

Will: Dad, please tell us a story with your mouth.

Connor: Yeah, Dad, please!

Dad: No guys. It's really late, and it has been a long week. I'm really tired, and we all need to get some sleep.

Will and Connor in unison: No, Dad. Just one story. With your mouth.

Dad: No guys. I'm just too tired tonight. I'll tell you an extra long story tomorrow night. I promise.

Will and Connor, again in unison: Please, Dad. Just one story. We can't go to sleep until you tell us a story.

Dad, sighing: Okay. But just a quick one.

Will and Connor, grinning with delight: Thanks, Dad.

Dad, again sighing: Let's see. A story. Hmmm, what do you want the story to be about?

Connor: A *Star Wars* story.

Dad: No, Connor. I am sick of telling you *Star Wars* stories.

Connor: Please, Dad. How about a story about Luke, Princess Leia, and Han Solo?

Dad: No, Connor. I've now told about three thousand Star Wars stories to you. Every variation possible. I've made up stories about Luke as a young boy. Luke as an old man. Luke in the next life. Luke in a previous life. I've told stories about Obi-Wan saving Yoda from Darth Vader. Yoda saving Obi-Wan from Darth Vader. And Darth Vader saving them both from the Evil Emperor. I've had Leia marrying Han, even Leia marrying Chewbacca! Why, George Lucas should hire me as a scriptwriter! I've worked out every possible plot imaginable for another *Star Wars* sequel, or prequel, or whatever it is they call *Star Wars* spin-offs these days.

Will: Who's George Lucas?

Dad: He's the guy who created *Star Wars*. Oh, never mind. Because it doesn't matter; I am not, repeat, NOT telling a *Star Wars* story tonight. I'll tell you a story about anything else in the world. But not *Star Wars*.

Connor: Okay.

Will: Okay already. You don't have to get all worked up.

Dad: So what do you want your story to be about?

Will and Connor, in unison: I don't know.

Dad: Come on. Make up something. The very first thing that comes into your mind.

Connor: A mole rat.

Dad: A mole rat? Where did you get that from?

Connor: We saw them at the zoo today on our field trip.

Dad: Okay. A mole rat it is. What shall we name the mole rat that'll be the star of our story?

Connor: Simon.

Dad: Why Simon?

Connor: I don't know. I could name him Squiggly.

Dad: No, Simon is fine. Let me tell you the story of "Simon the Mole Rat." This is a very special story. Do you know what makes this story so special?

Will and Connor, again in unison: I don't know, Dad. What makes this story so special?

Dad: Let me tell you. Once upon a time . . .

Courtesy of Deena Gorland Photography

About the Authors

William and Connor McCormick reside with their mother, Danna, and their father and co-author, John, in Washington, D.C., U.S.A. Will and Connor are elementary school students at the Sheridan School in Washington, D.C. Danna is a web developer and owns her own company, DLM Web Development. John is an attorney practicing in Washington, D.C. (Also pictured is the family's beloved bulldog, Spencer.)

This is Will, Connor, and John's first book.

For more information about storytelling with children, visit www.DadTellMeAStory.com.

LaVergne, TN USA
26 November 2010
205976LV00003BA